Murder in the 11th House

Books by Mitchell Scott Lewis

Murder in the 11th House

Murder in the 11th House

A Starlight Detective Agency Mystery

Mitchell Scott Lewis

Poisoned Pen Press

First Edition 2011

10 9 8 7 6 5 4 3 2 1

Library of Congress Catalog Card Number: 2011926961

ISBN: 9781590589502 Hardcover
9781590589526 Trade Paperback

Poisoned Pen Press
6962 E. First Ave., Ste. 103
Scottsdale, AZ 85251
www.poisonedpenpress.com
info@poisonedpenpress.com

Printed in the United States of America

*For my father,
a wonderful writer.*

Acknowledgments

To my agent, Sandra Bond with deepest gratitude. To Barbara Peters, Robert Rosenwald, and Jessica Tribble at Poisoned Pen Press for your wonderful advice and insights, and for taking a chance on a new voice. Thank you so much.

To my dear friend, Fiona Druckenmiller; words can never express my humble gratitude for your unwavering friendship, faith, and support. Thank you from the bottom of my heart. To Roberta Cary, for your generous understanding and wisdom. And to Natalie Lico, for your steadfast camaraderie and affection.

And finally, to Carl Lennertz, my editor, teacher, sparring partner and friend, without whom this work simply would never have existed. Your vision and talents are awe-inspiring. And your Job-like patience allowed me to make a dream come true. I will never be able to thank you enough. I am forever in your debt.

The man is nothing. The work is all.
—French proverb

Chapter One

David Lowell was up before five. He left his townhouse on East Ninety-third Street and walked out into the darkness. Only Wall Streeters headed for the subway and diner workers serving the first coffee were up this early. Although it was an unseasonably mild November, the early morning chill forced him to pull the collar of his leather jacket up around his neck. He left his ponytail tucked in.

It was late autumn, and most of the trees had long since lost their flamboyant costumes. A few luminous oaks and maples had stubbornly refused to relinquish their bright skirts and stood out strikingly against a canvas of aging brick and cold steel. He touched the hair around his ears, his own foliage, faded grey from so many turns on the merry-go-round. *How drab is humankind,* he thought, *so unadorned in its final days. Not gallantly lit up like autumn leaves, a brief colorful flair of brilliance against death's pale pallet, but washed out and ominous, like the sky before a coming storm. No thought of the inevitable spring, only of the seemingly endless winter.*

He needed to take a long walk. Lost in his thoughts, he strolled from the Upper East Side all the way to Soho, the dark city passing in a fog. He walked up and down the city's subtle hills as he made his way south. He crossed Spring Street and went down to Canal where he turned left and passed jewelry stores and knock-off purse kiosks. Most were still closed, their barren metal gates stark and uninviting, but a few enterprising souls were already open for business, maybe hoping for a flush insomniac tourist.

He swung onto Elizabeth and headed north again. The city had changed so much in the past decade it was hardly the same New York. Rezoning, overexpansion, and the continued demise of rent-stabilization had changed the face of Manhattan neighborhoods seemingly overnight. Except for Chinatown, which stubbornly tried to keep its ethnic barriers in place, there were no neighborhoods anymore. Not in the traditional sense. This area was still called Little Italy and had once been the center of communities transplanted from Naples and Rome and the refuge of the "families." For almost a century, apartments in this neighborhood were rarely robbed and parked cars were hardly ever broken into for fear of retribution. But now walk-ups rented for three thousand a month, and there were more upwardly mobile financiers and rich out-of-towners than tough-looking men in gray suits and old women sitting on stoops trading recipes.

He continued to stroll uptown toward his destination, walking slowly and methodically. Gradually the city awoke and people spilled out of the buildings onto the roads and sidewalks. He meandered through midtown, jostled by commuters and harried employees hustling to work, most glad to still have a job.

At the corner of Twenty-fourth Street, he stopped into a deli for some pre-cut fresh melon and a corn muffin to get him through the morning's paperwork and phone calls. He had picked up a donut but put it back down with a sigh.

Leaving the store and turning down the side street, he went into the second building, took the elevator up to the sixth floor, entered the offices of the Starlight Detective Agency and began his day.

The prospective client, arriving promptly for his afternoon appointment, was a tall nervous man, almost totally bald. His large misshapen nose twitched repeatedly. He shouldered into the office, pushing through the mahogany door hard enough to make it to bang against the wall.

"May I help you, sir?" Stationed at the reception desk, Sarah unconsciously pushed her bright red hair back behind her ears in preparation for battle.

"Is *this* a detective agency?" He let the question fly with disdain.

"That's what the sign says, unless the business changed overnight." Sarah couldn't resist the wisecrack delivered with a big smile. She was used to the type of clientele her boss attracted, and this guy wasn't going to get her goat.

"What the hell kind of name is Starlight Detective Agency, anyway?"

"Do you have an appointment, sir?"

"An appointment? Yeah, yeah, I made an appointment. Name's Waldo Jefferson. A friend recommended your company, said this guy's some sort of genius. But I'm beginning to have my doubts."

He looked around at the office, its Spartan decorations rather dreary-looking, save for the fresh flowers that Sarah brought in every few days. She was amused when he actually ran his finger across her desk looking for dust. She thought people only did that in the movies.

"What a dump," he said.

"I like it." She beamed again. "Anyway, yes, Mr. Jefferson, you are scheduled for 1:00. If you'll just have a seat, Mr. Lowell will be with you in a few moments. Would you like some coffee while you wait?"

"Huh? Coffee? No thank you."

Sarah got up to close the door, and returned to her typing.

Jefferson walked over to the couch, sat, and fidgeted.

"Listen," he said, "I'm having second thoughts about this."

Just then the door to the inner office opened and David Lowell exited with an elderly woman, her frail hand holding his arm for support.

The woman was drying her eyes. "Oh," she said, her voice quivering, "I can't thank you enough. I'm just glad to put closure to all this mess."

Lowell smiled empathetically, and patted her hand. "The truth is always better. It will free you from all your burdens."

"It will, and thank you, you dear man." She got up on her tiptoes and kissed him on the cheek, then exited.

"Dearest Sarah, what's up next?" Lowell tugged on his neatly-tied salt-and-pepper ponytail. Although not quite five-nine, his bearing and body language gave the impression of a taller man.

"Mr. Jefferson is here to see you." She tilted her head toward the couch, her eyebrows lifting.

"Ah, Mr. Jefferson, yes. David Lowell. Please, come in, come in."

Lowell pointed the way to the inner office. Just before disappearing, Lowell turned and gave Sarah a wink, a tacit *thank you* for her patience with the client.

Sarah winked back as the inner door closed with a click.

Lowell walked around his huge desk, gesturing toward the two large, leather chairs.

"Now Mr. Jefferson, what can I do for you?" Lowell sat after his client seated himself.

"You were recommended by a friend, Jake Lerner," he grunted.

"Yes, Mr. Lerner. I did some work for him a few years back, and he was quite satisfied, as I recall. I trust you will be as well." Lowell turned toward a computer screen and began typing.

"Well, that remains to be seen. My problem is a bit more complex than Lerner's. You see my wife is missing…"

"What's your birthday?"

"I beg your pardon?"

"Your birthday. Date, month, year."

"Well, I ah, that is…June 14th, 1948. But for God's sake what does that have to do with anything."

"Hmm, born around noon, I would guess."

"At 12:17 P.M. to be exact," Jefferson replied, obviously annoyed.

"Of course," Lowell said, looking at the man's features, "a Capricorn ascendant." He studied the screen for a moment. "Ah, you've got a T-Square with the Moon in Virgo, squaring Jupiter on one side, and the Sun-Uranus conjunct on the other. You've got quite a temper, haven't you? It probably stems from your parents' relationship and their ultimate divorce."

"What the hell is this, astrology?"

"I thought you knew my technique, Mr. Jefferson. Didn't Mr. Lerner tell you?"

Jefferson jerked his hands up off his knees and slapped them back down. "Oh, my God! I'm in a nut house."

"Mr. Jefferson, I assure you that I am just as sane as you. Perhaps more so, now that I see your chart." Lowell chuckled and pulled on his ponytail again.

"This is great. I've got a missing wife, two screaming kids, and Lerner sends me to a psychic Sherlock-freaking-Holmes."

The detective snorted. "If you must compare me to a fictional character I would much prefer Sherlock-freaking-Holmes' brother, Mycroft, the intelligent member of that family. *He* never had to deal with the public."

"I didn't know Sherlock Holmes even had a brother."

"Nasty and illiterate, nice combination." Lowell regarded him steadily.

"This is too much. I'm leaving."

"I figured you would." Lowell looked down at the man's natal chart. "But before you go let me just tell you. Your wife isn't missing; she ran away from you with a man who is more likely than not an Aquarian or a Leo. It is someone you've known for a long time, whom you considered a friend. You may hear from her around the full moon on the tenth. You are a brutish and cruel man who pushed her to this. She should have left you years ago."

"Why you… I should sue you."

Lowell barged ahead. "You also seem to have a problem with your kidneys; probably a susceptibility to recurring infections. Venus squares Neptune in the natal chart. It should manifest again in the next few months. Also you may have a heart attack in about eighteen months if you don't deal with your blood pressure. Whether it is fatal or not has to do with you and your attitude. The Sun-Uranus conjunct shows a propensity toward heart trouble or strokes, and you are about to have some difficult aspects."

"I didn't ask you…"

"When you were about seven, your parents divorced and you lived with your father until his death, when you were around twenty-one. After that you probably lived alone until your marriage. You never forgave your mother for deserting you, and you have taken it out on every woman who has been unfortunate enough to come into your circle."

Jefferson's face had turned bright red. His breathing was short and, as he tried to stand, he had to steady himself against the arm of the large chair. "How could you know all that?"

"Of course, all of this is just a guess, and should not be misconstrued as a diagnosis or an opinion."

Jefferson got up from the chair, never taking his eyes off of Lowell. "You're the devil," he said, as he headed for the door.

"There's no charge for this visit. Good day."

Jefferson opened the inner door and strode quickly through the small waiting area.

Sarah looked up from her computer. "Shall I make you another appointment?"

Jefferson's turned back to her, his eyes opened wide. Shaking his head, he grabbed the carved knob of the door, pulled it open and rushed out into the hallway, rudely leaving the door open.

Sarah shrugged, got up, gently closed the door, then came back to her desk and called in an order for a late lunch for two.

◇◇◇

When Sarah brought lunch in, Lowell was sitting at his oversized desk engrossed in his work, his head bowed. Three computer screens sat on top, and all were aglow. Against the far wall on a wooden console, a TV was muted and set to CNBC. Stock and commodity quotes passed unceasingly across the bottom of the screen.

"Where should I put it?" said Sarah.

He picked his head up. "Oh, I don't care. Put it on the table." Then he put his head back down.

Sarah had been working at Starlight Detective Agency for about three years. Her boss was snobbish and demanding. And he was the smartest man she had ever met. He also paid her more than twice what she might have made anywhere else.

The workload wasn't anything she couldn't handle. True, there was the occasional extra job that required her to impersonate someone or engage in some leg work, which had so far resulted in her being shot at several times and almost run over once. But each time she had been well compensated for her efforts. He was a little strange, and his friends and clients tended toward the unusual, but considering the uniqueness of the situation, it wasn't as bizarre as it could have been.

Maybe working for an astrological detective in New York qualified her for some sort of reality show. She'd look into that.

She put the food on the coffee table and returned to her desk.

Lowell stood up, stretched and went over to the table. He had been engrossed in his work for hours and had forgotten about lunch. He unwrapped the wax paper and walked over to the window with half the sandwich. He leaned over a glass tank and spoke to two large black and red turtles.

"Hello, Buster," he said to the first, as it stuck its head out for a noon scratch. The second lumbered toward his outstretched finger and received its reward. "Hello, Keaton," he said to the second. They were red-eared sliders he had bought on Canal Street when he opened the offices. The size of his thumb when he got them, they were now each a foot in length and growing. They would soon need a bigger home.

He gave them some of his sandwich and went back to his desk, picked up the phone, and hit speed dial #3.

"Solomon Smith Barney," said a female voice. "I mean Citi Smith Barney... oops, Morgan Stanley." A big sigh. "I'm sorry, who do you want?"

"Roger Bowman," said Lowell.

A moment later, a man came on the line. "This is Roger."

"It's David Lowell."

"Hey, Starman, when are you coming down to say hello?"

"Soon. What do you see in the metals?"

"The spreads look a bit bearish, as does the daily moving average."

"I'm getting a strong sell signal as we head into the waning moon."

"You getting out?"

"Yes," replied Lowell, a mouthful of sandwich muffling his response. He swallowed. "Sorry, I haven't had time to stop for lunch all day. I'm going to flatten my position. The New Moon on Sunday is void of course, so I would look for a false run-up the early part of the week. After it drops again you should buy —sometime around Thursday."

"I don't know what the hell you're talking about, as usual. But if you're getting out, so am I."

Lowell laughed.

"On tomorrow's open, I want you to sell ten December gold at the market and twenty December silver, and buy fifty November beans market with a stop at, hold on a minute," he grabbed a piece of paper, "put the stop at twelve-forty."

Roger repeated the order for confirmation.

"Done. I'll email you the fills."

"Thanks, Roger. We'll have lunch soon, I promise. Oh, and please send half of this month's profits to the ASPCA, as usual. Thanks."

He hung up and worked for a while, occasionally nibbling at his sandwich until the intercom buzzed.

He picked up the phone. "Yes, Sarah, what is it?"

"You have a visitor."

"I'm much too busy to see anyone without an appointment. And it's getting near the end of the day."

He clicked off the intercom and went back to work. It buzzed again.

"Yes, Sarah, what is it this time?"

"You, uh that is, um…"

Lowell sighed. "All right, Sarah," he sighed, "send them in."

The door opened and a woman entered. She smiled and nodded at him and then walked over to the turtle tank without saying a word.

Lowell turned his swivel chair around and watched her.

She was so beautiful, standing there next to the window, the afternoon sun blazing around her dark brown hair like an angel's aura. She looked out the window at the unobstructed view of the Empire State Building glistening in the distance, so magnificent, so unreal.

"I always loved this view," she said. "It makes me feel like I'm inside a postcard, or one of those things you shake to make snow."

She absently petted the turtles.

She turned and faced him.

She looks older, he thought, *more mature, more distinguished.*

At five-eleven, she carried herself with a graceful-awkwardness. Her pinstriped business suit looked new.

They both remained mute, the silence quite maddening to Lowell.

Finally she said: "I want to hire you."

"That's it? No hello?"

"Hello, Dad," she smiled. "I want to hire you."

Chapter Two

The suite of offices that housed the Starlight Detective Agency consisted of the reception area and three private offices: one for Lowell; another for Mort, his assistant; and one they used as a conference room.

Lowell's office had a large private bathroom with an oversized tub and shower and a compact but completely modern kitchen hidden behind one of the doors. While on a case, Lowell would often spend several days and nights here so he wouldn't be distracted. The couch was a pull-out with a king-size orthopedic mattress.

Lowell looked at his watch and then got up to take his coffee cup to the kitchen.

Melinda watched her father walk across the room. "You're wearing a turtleneck color I haven't seen before. And your jeans look new, too."

Lowell had a wardrobe that consisted of three dozen different turtlenecks of various colors and fabric weight. And he wore jeans that, against all convention, he had pressed with a sharp crease down the front and back. His shoes were always loafers. He hated laces.

Lowell looked down, and gave out a sigh. "Yes, I had to give in and buy some jeans one size larger. It was painful to do. But enough chatter. I'm done for the day, Melinda. If you don't have plans, why don't you join me for dinner at home and you can tell me about the case?"

"You think I have no plans, dad? I'm a very busy woman."

"He sighed. "I know. Maybe you could indulge your lonely father."

"I'm teasing you. I would love to go uptown. I could use a bottle of beer from your precious collection. You still have my favorite, Old Peculiar?"

"I am trying to drink less beer and more red wine. For my health." Lowell smiled, made a quick call, turned off his computers, and grabbed his leather jacket.

Outside, a black limo was idling and a guy straight out of a "Join the Marines" commercial stood alongside.

"Hello, Andy." Melinda smiled at the driver her father had hired a few years ago after a particularly threatening case.

"Melinda, how nice to see you." Andy tipped his hat slightly.

Melinda noticed the bulge of the holster under the left arm of Andy's suit jacket and shuddered slightly. She hoped the case she had to tell her father about wouldn't require hardware.

Twenty minutes later they were sitting in the backyard of his townhouse on Ninety-third Street. Lowell had installed high walls made of wide pine slabs on three sides to guarantee at least a modicum of privacy in a very public city. Although Melinda always felt like she was sitting in a cardboard box, it formed a pleasant hideaway in Manhattan. The garden that circled the patio was always beautifully planted by Julia, Lowell's live-in housekeeper, who considered it her own private piece of earth and tended it with loving care.

It was a beautiful November evening, although still quite warm. They both had taken their jackets off and draped them over the high-backed wrought-iron chairs that sat around a round glass-topped table.

David cracked the screw-top on a bottle of merlot, inserted an aerating spout, and poured them each a glass.

"Father, screw-tops? You?"

"I am changing with the times, and there is less spoilage than on the cork." Lowell sampled the wine and savored it for a moment. "And how have you been?"

"I've been okay, dad. You look a little tired."

He laughed. "Strange case. Sad case, too. Today is my first day in weeks back to a semblance of normal."

"I read about it in the papers. So rich, so famous, yet it still didn't help, did it?"

"Even the rich can die horrible deaths."

She nodded.

"And speaking of money..." he said, reaching for his wallet.

"I don't need any more money," she barked. "I happen to make a living. And I wish you'd stop putting it into my checking account. I've changed banks three times and you still find me. How do you do it?"

He remained motionless.

"It's Mort, isn't it? He hacks in and finds my new accounts. Well, cut it out. I don't need your money and I don't want it."

"But it's all for you anyway. That's why I earned it, for you kids, and your mother."

"Well she's perfectly happy to take it. Why don't you just give her my share?"

He sighed. "You know, money isn't good or evil. It's what you do with it that decides."

"Maybe, but I haven't seen it do much good in my line of work."

She looked at her father. He was thick and sturdy, built like a wrestler. But he was showing just the beginnings of a slight paunch.

"Where's Julia?" Melinda asked.

"Night off. Now, tell me about the case."

"Well, my client is Johnny Colbert, a bartender with no money. It's pro bono, and since I'm the most junior associate..."

"...you got assigned it. It'll be good experience. So what have you got for me?"

She pulled a manila envelope from her bag, opened it and handed him a few pages.

"Here is the birth chart: born January 26, 1971, at 5:31 P.M. in Stewville, Indiana."

Lowell picked up the astrology chart and began scrutinizing it.

"What do you think?" asked his daughter. "Anything unusual about it?

"Actually, I think this is a very unusual and quite active chart. This is certainly a person of high energy and with a possible duality in the personality."

"Is there anything that stands out, or surprises you?"

"Remember, there are limits to what a birth chart can show you."

"I understand," said Melinda, with some disappointment.

"For example, it doesn't necessarily tell me that 'Johnny' Colbert is a woman, probably born Joanna or Jeannie."

Melinda perked up.

"But how..."

"A combination of things. For one thing, what I read as a dual personality may very well manifest as a male who is too female or a female who is too male. The inner pressure this person feels may very well be a result of his sexual identity, but it in no way implies his sexual orientation. A woman with this chart would have to contend with the contradictions and aggressive personality this would create, and may decide to take a traditionally male name."

He sipped his wine.

"But mostly I knew Johnny was a girl because of you."

"Me?"

"Of course. How you acted. Your insistence that there *was* something hidden made me view things from a slightly different perspective. And once I did that it became fairly obvious. Besides, it has always been tempting for you to test me in such a childish manner."

"Oh, dad."

"What's she charged with?"

"Killing a judge. Two days ago. It's all over the papers. You really have been out of touch."

Lowell put the astrology chart down.

"Killing a judge? What judge?"

"I don't think you knew her. Her name was Farrah Winston."

"No, I never heard of her. What court?"

"Debt claims. Lower Manhattan."

"Hmm, I'm guessing a Republican."

"That's right. How did you…"

"Wasn't she a little young to be a judge?"

"Now how could you possibly…oh I see," said Melinda, nodding her head. "Farrah didn't come into popularity as a girl's name until the mid seventies, when Farrah Fawcett was a star, so she would only be in her thirties. And since she is so young, unless she was recently named to the bench you're assuming she had to be appointed within the twelve years that the governor was a Republican, ergo…"

"That's my girl."

She smiled at the condescending accolade despite herself.

"You'll notice," she pointed to the client's chart, "that Johnny has a stellium in Sagittarius with Mars in between Jupiter and Neptune. Wouldn't you think she flips between ego grandiosity and terrible self-doubt?"

"I think that's a very good analysis of those aspects."

"So, do you think she has the ego to murder someone?"

"If it were only that simple. Anyone can murder given the right motivation and circumstances. The chart may tell us how they would go about doing it."

Lowell picked up the chart again and pointed.

"She may not have the ego, but she certainly has the temper. See, she's got Mercury and Uranus in a very tight square, showing a very explosive side to her personality. This is quite a complicated chart. First of all, there is that potent conjunct in Sagittarius, with the three planets extraordinarily close together. This shows great potential. The world was immersed in a rare and powerful moment on the days surrounding her birth. There are probably quite a number of her immediate contemporaries just waiting to explode. Some will do great things, others may do terrible things. But there's much more here to consider."

"Tell me."

"Well," he continued, "she is a Dark of the Moon baby, born in Aquarius right before the New Moon. What does that tell you?"

"That she's always trying to finish up things or catch up to herself."

"Right. What else?"

"She hides a lot of stuff."

He nodded. "Exactly. There's no light. It was literally dark when she was born, just before the new moon, and she lives her life in the shadows. Nobody really knows what she's thinking until she decides to share it."

"Someone else has that configuration in Aquarius. I remember looking at a chart recently. Who was it?"

"Our mayor."

"Oh yes, how could I forget? You did a lecture on his political aspirations last year."

"You were there?"

She laughed. "Sure. Sitting in the back where I hoped you couldn't see me. You don't mind, do you?"

"No. I'm glad you were there."

"It was a great lecture," said his daughter, with real pride.

Lowell almost smiled. "Okay, so Ms. Colbert has a hidden agenda. Let's go see her tomorrow and try and find out what that is."

Chapter Three

Riker's Island is a dark and cold place and, Lowell felt, made to look even more sinister than was necessary. He pitied the poor bastards without enough money for bail. Even the innocent were forced to stay in this hell hole for weeks, or even months, awaiting justice if they lacked funds. Even crueler, guests of the prison had a clear view of LaGuardia Airport, so they got to see and hear free folks jetting around the world at their leisure 24/7. Lowell thought that a choice between another plane trip and a day in lock-up might be a toss-up for him, and jail food might be better.

Being the attorney of record and by arriving first thing in the morning, Melinda got them in quickly. They sat silently in a small, bare room with a metal table and four chairs. After a few minutes the door opened and a female guard led the client in, and then stood at the door out of earshot but quite present.

"Hello, Johnny," said Melinda. "This is my father."

"How do you do," said Lowell.

"Not so great at the moment," replied Johnny, as she sat. A tattoo of a lion's tail was visible under her sleeve, as was the result of hundreds of hours in the gym.

"Did you kill her?" asked Lowell.

"Father!"

"Well, did you? I haven't got all day to waste if you're guilty."

Johnny got red in the face. She stood up and leaned over the table. The guard made a move in their direction. Lowell held up his hand and waved the guard back.

"Fuck you," Johnny said. "I never hurt anyone in my life who wasn't trying to hurt me first."

"Maybe so, but you've got a temper. Sit down."

Johnny sat.

"Yes, I do," she said, breathing deeply and trying to regain her composure.

Lowell turned to his daughter. "I had to see it upfront."

"I'm sorry," said Johnny. "I don't usually lose it so quickly. You try keeping your cool in a cellblock with fifty psychotic women screaming all the time. I haven't slept since I got here."

Lowell picked up Johnny's chart and showed it to Melinda. "Remember, Mercury squares Uranus, giving her a sharp tongue. She's nervous, impetuous, and probably accident-prone. Ever hurt your ankles?" he asked her.

"Yeah, as a matter of fact I did when I was a kid. Cracked my left ankle so bad I couldn't play sports much. It never healed properly. It still gives me trouble if I stand too long in one place. Great injury for a bartender, huh?"

"Car accident?"

"Yeah, my father was driving and some asshole cut us off. I slammed into the windshield and twisted my leg, breaking the bones."

Lowell turned to his daughter.

"Mercury rules cars," said Melinda.

"And?"

"And Uranus rules the ankles as well as sudden events."

Lowell smiled.

"So, you're like, an astrologist?" asked Johnny.

"I prefer astrologer."

"Wow. This shit really works? Can you fucking believe it?"

Lowell frowned.

"All right, so let's say you didn't do it. You were in her courtroom two days before she was killed. Why?"

"I was being sued by several collection agencies."

"Several?"

"I got into some financial difficulty over the last few years and couldn't get out from under, that's all."

"And there was some trouble in the court?"

"I, uh, well that is... I pretty much accused her of taking bribes from the collection agencies and she didn't take too kindly to my ideas. The bitch cited me for contempt and put me in lockup for the rest of the day."

"Was your language liberally peppered with expletives?"

"What?"

"My father wants to know if you were swearing in front of the judge," said Melinda.

"Oh, fuck no. I show respect when it's called for. At least I did until those rat bastards started snowballing me."

Lowell shook his head. "This wasn't the first time you were in front of Judge Winston?"

"No. I was in her courtroom three other times before. I owed money on a lot of credit cards."

"So what made you accuse her this time?"

Johnny rubbed her neck and stretched. "I don't know. I was hung over and hadn't slept much. And she was just letting them get away with all sorts of illegal bullshit and I just didn't feel like taking it anymore."

"We'll get to that later." He picked up the chart. "After you got yourself into financial difficulty you tried to bail yourself out. But it didn't work out the way you planned, did it?"

"I don't know what you mean?"

"What you really did was give in to your problem, didn't you?"

"Problem," said Melinda, "what problem?"

"I don't know what you're talking about," said Johnny.

Lowell picked up the client's birth chart and turned to his daughter.

"Jupiter rules the 5th House," he began, pointing at the paper, "and it is conjunct Mars and Neptune. What does that tell you that might be pertinent here?"

Melinda thought for a moment and then turned to her client. "A gambling problem?"

"What," Johnny protested, "I don't..."

Lowell put the file down softly.

"Okay, maybe it's true. I think I do have a little bit of a gambling problem. But I never did before. It just sort of snuck up on me. My whole life it was rare if I even bet a football pool or put money on a game. As a bartender, I found it much easier to let them bet with each other. That way whoever won tipped me pretty good. But it's just impossible to make a living in this city anymore, and I had to do something to make ends meet, so I thought I could win some."

"You always had a gambling problem waiting to surface," said Lowell, "it just never manifested before."

"Yeah, whatever."

"Did you ever win?"

"Of course I did. What, do you think I'm an idiot? The first time I played, I won five hundred bucks. It paid the electric and cable bills. I won five thousand once, right before Christmas, that was cool, and fifteen hundred, and five hundred a few more times."

"And in the end?"

"I don't know, I never added it up."

Lowell looked her in the eyes. "What do you think?"

She rubbed her eyes and sighed. "What the hell difference does it make? I don't know. My whole life is cash. Whatever is in my pocket is what's real. I don't think about where it goes, only where I can get some more."

Lowell said nothing.

"Oh, Christ, I suppose I must have lost in the long run. But what are you supposed to do? You got like three hundred bucks in your pocket and you owe three grand. You got to try something."

She put her fingers on her temples as if for support and slowly shook her head, her short blond bangs swaying with the motion. "You got to try something."

Then she put her head down on the desk and moaned. "I got a fucking headache you wouldn't believe."

"Johnny," said Melinda, "why don't you tell us the whole story from the beginning."

She picked her head up with obvious concerted effort.

"I used to make a fairly good living as a bartender. I paid my bills, had a small retirement fund, and even started putting something away for a small house upstate. I've worked on my feet for almost twenty years. But then things started to change.

"First 9/11 happened. Business took a dive. My income shrank, but I survived that. Then they outlawed smoking in bars. People wouldn't stay as long or run up as high a tab. Some went outside to smoke and never came back to pay the bill. It was a real mess. But I was able to keep my head above water somehow. Finally this stupid recession hit. It became impossible for me to continue paying my bills and making payments on the credit cards, so I just stopped."

Lowell listened intently. "Go on,"

"It was Wednesday, the day before Thanksgiving," continued the client. "I was going to Boston to visit some friends and went to Penn Station to take Amtrak. The place was mobbed, as you can imagine, but I could only get two days off and had to travel on that day. I didn't mind. I enjoy face surfing, anyway."

"Face what?' interrupted Lowell.

"Face surfing. You know, walking through a crowd and glancing at all the different faces, jumping from one to another, like surfing the waves. Face surfing."

"Ah. Continue."

"I didn't want to stand on line for an hour, so I used an automated ticket machine. When I put in my debit card it was rejected, saying I had insufficient funds. I knew I had enough money, having deposited five hundred bucks the day before. I didn't know what to do. I had no choice but to stand on line and wait for a ticket agent and try to pay by check. When I finally got to the window she refused to take my check because the address on the check was different than on my license. I had moved and never told the motor vehicle bureau."

Lowell raised his eyebrows.

"Helps keep you off jury duty," said the client.

"Then what happened?"

"The supervisor refused my check as well, and I left the station."

"Voluntarily?"

"Escorted by two of New York's finest. Although I usually am a very quiet person I do have a temper, as you now know. I had made these plans months in advance and now I wasn't going to be able to see my people. It pissed me off."

"Then what happened?"

"I had no money and couldn't go. I wound up eating a baked potato and some leftover salad for my Thanksgiving dinner."

"So then what did you do?"

"I was mad as hell. I'd been sued before, but this time they didn't even let me know. They just grabbed my money."

"So you went to court."

"Armed with the truth and what was left of my dignity. I got there at nine a.m. and sat with the rest of the losers waiting my turn. When my case was called I got up and walked to the front and stood in front of the judge."

"Judge Winston?"

Johnny and Melinda both nodded.

"It usually takes a lot to make me angry. That's why I've been able to work as a bartender in Manhattan for so long. Maybe it was exhaustion, or maybe it was the circumstances, but I just lost it. I told the judge that this is bullshit. I asked her: '*Are you telling me that you have no intention of making these people answer for their actions*?'"

"What did she do?"

"The judge kept saying '*do you owe them the money or don't you*?' over and over again. It was really getting on my nerves."

"So what did you do?"

"Finally I shouted at her something like: '*Do you work on a commission, or are you on a monthly retainer*?'"

"And then?"

"She picked up her gavel and pointed it at me and said: '*Are you saying what I think you're saying? Because if you are, you're going to spend the rest of the day and maybe the weekend in jail. Would you like that? Now, do you owe them the money?*' That's when I finally lost it altogether. Nothing I could do to hold it back. It's been that way my whole life. Pretty hard to anger, but harder to stop. So I shouted out '*I don't owe them, or you, a rat's fucking ass.*'"

"Yes, your colorful language. I assume she didn't take too kindly to your remarks."

"She slammed the gavel down on her desk three times and then told the bailiff to escort me to lockup."

"According to the court papers, you threatened to kill Judge Winston."

"Yeah, well sort of."

"What do you mean, *sort of?*"

"As we were heading out the door I turned back to the judge and shouted: '*You fucking asshole, I'll kill you.*' But I didn't mean it. I was just mad, you know?"

"So she threw you in jail," said Lowell, "and held you in contempt of court for the rest of the day."

"Yep," said Johnny.

"I've had to deal with those courts for years," said Melinda. "It's disgraceful what goes on. It's almost enough to make you wonder if they *aren't* all in it together."

"You see? Maybe I'm not so wrong after all."

Melinda tried to soften her criticism. "It's possible, but I think for the most part it's just a lousy system that doesn't work all that well. When there is enough incompetence, you don't need corruption."

"Did you kill Judge Farrah Winston?" asked Lowell a second time.

"No," said Johnny, in a quiet voice, "I've never killed anyone."

"Where were you the afternoon she was murdered?"

"I was home alone. I have no alibi."

"One more question. What did you gamble on? Horses? Poker?"

"State lottery," she said.

"Oh, my God," said Lowell. "Not lotto."

Johnny nodded.

"Lotto, daily numbers, Take Five, all of them. And scratch-off tickets. Lots and lots of scratch-off tickets."

"What kind of tickets?" asked Lowell.

"Scratch-off. You know. New York State lottery scratch-off tickets?"

Lowell shook his head. "Sorry, I'm not familiar with them."

Johnny looked at Melinda and tilted her head.

Melinda smiled and turned toward her father. "You really do live in your own world, don't you?"

He stood. "All right, I'll look into your case."

The others stood.

This time Johnny stuck out her hand. "You're her father? Are you doing this as a favor to your kid, or are you for real?"

"I'm not doing this as a favor."

"Then I want to thank you. I knew I was very lucky to get Ms. Lowell as a lawyer, and with your help I'm sure you can clear me."

"Well," said Lowell, receiving her surprisingly robust grip, "let's not get ahead of ourselves. We'll be in touch."

"You know where to find me."

Chapter Four

The office was stuffy. Lowell opened the windows and turned on the overhead fan. He went to the refrigerator and took out a bottle of sparkling water.

"Want anything?"

"No, thanks," said Melinda. "So what do you think?

They hadn't talked on the ride back from Riker's.

He unscrewed the cap and took a long swig from the bottle. "I don't know yet."

"But you're willing to look into it."

"I promised you I would, and I will."

Melinda walked over to the turtles and offered her finger. They both waddled toward her. "I feel badly that she has to stay in that awful place. It's a dreadful thing to be locked up like that. Did you see how pale she was?"

"That could be her natural pallor for all we know."

"I don't think so. Besides, with her aggressive personality, I'm worried for her safety. Bail is set at one million dollars. There's no way she can ever raise that kind of money."

Lowell put the bottle down on his desk. "What would you like me to do, pay her bail?"

"Really, would you?"

"No."

His daughter stood with her mouth partially open.

"You'd just let her sit…"

"For all we know she *did* kill Judge Winston."

"You don't believe that for a minute."

He shrugged.

"You just don't like her attitude. You're such a snob."

"Thank you."

"Oh, Dad…"

He smiled as he picked up the intercom.

"Sarah, would you bring in two coffees?"

"Sure, boss."

As Sarah poured coffee into two mugs, a little spilled onto one of her shoes. She gasped audibly, took a napkin and bent down, holding her breath the whole time. These weren't regular shoes that one would find in Macy's. These were Italian, hand-made of the softest leather. And they cost Sarah much more than she could afford.

Luckily the coffee droplet came right up and left no stain. She let her breath out. She had a closet full of expensive footwear that she fawned over and treated as one would a pet or a child.

Sarah had a problem with shoes.

Relieved, she took the coffee cups by the handles in one hand, opened the door, and entered the inner sanctum.

"Hey, boss."

She saw Melinda.

"Hi," she said, in a friendly voice. "Nice to see you, Melinda. We didn't get much of a chance to say hello before. How are things?"

"Not bad. How are you, Sarah?"

"Well, we had some excitement in the past month or so. But I'm sure you know." She handed Melinda a cup and then Lowell.

"Yes, I heard a little about it."

"Sarah," said Lowell, "I want you to do an errand for me."

"Sure, what can I do?"

Lowell pulled out his wallet.

"You're a bit of a gambler. I want you to go to the deli on the corner and buy me some scratch-off tickets."

"Boss?"

"It's for a case."

"Okay. What kind?"

"I don't know, is there more than one variety?"

"Dozens," replied Sarah.

"Well," he handed her two one hundred-dollar bills, "just pick up a nice selection."

"Okay."

She took the money and left.

Melinda was feeding the turtles. "What's next?"

"Let me get Mort in here to do a little research for me." He picked up the intercom phone and pushed #1. A faint buzz came through the wall. "Let's see if he's in. I never know the hours he keeps."

"He's really good, isn't he?" asked Melinda.

"One of the best hackers in the business. In fact, Mort was asked to leave MIT after he used their computer to hack into secret government files. It would have been too embarrassing to prosecute him, so the government offered him a job in their computer section, which he turned down, and now he works for the Starlight Detective Agency."

"He seems like such a nice man to be doing such unusual things."

Lowell laughed. "He's unusual enough. I've known him since my days on Wall Street, when we both lived in Battery Park City. He was eking out a living giving psychic readings when we met."

"Was he any good?"

"Actually, yes. I find his predictions about the future to be amazingly accurate at times. Although like most good psychics, he has difficulty with timing things. And he does have an uncanny ability to read people's emotions."

"Can he read yours?"

"What do you think?"

"I think if he could, you wouldn't have hired him. You're much too private a person."

Lowell swiveled in his chair to face his daughter.

"Seeing anyone special?"

"Not really."

"Whatever happened with, uh…"

"Peter. His name is Peter. I dated him for almost two years. You could at least remember his name."

"Right, Peter. Whatever happened with him?"

"You mean the same Peter that neither you nor mother ever spent a second talking to? Is that the Peter you're asking about?"

"Well, I…"

"We broke up."

"Ah."

"Are you happy about it?"

"No, why should I be happy about it? I only want what's best for you and makes you happy."

"You know, that's almost word-for-word what Mom said."

"Even if we're not together we often see eye to eye on things."

The door opened and Mort entered.

"Good morning, David, what's up? Melinda, what a nice surprise."

He walked over to Melinda and kissed her on the cheek.

"How's Peter?"

"At least someone remembers his name."

Mort stepped back. "You broke up. I'm sorry."

Melinda smiled. "You're very right," she told the psychic. "Good call."

He curled his face into a most unnatural scowl, wrinkling his nose and puckering his brow, as he did whenever he made a prediction. "It was the right thing to do. You're going to find someone else very soon. Someone much better for you. I feel a "B" or a "V" in the name."

She smiled and patted him on the shoulder. "Thank you, I needed to hear that."

"Is this a social visit?" he asked, relaxing his face.

"I'm afraid not. I have a client in need of your firm's rather unique skills."

"Always glad to help anyone you feel deserves our attention. Okay, what can I do?"

Lowell pulled several pieces of paper from his printer tray and handed them to Mort. "You can begin by telling me everything you can find out about these people. The first is the victim, a judge from debtor's court. The second is our client, a bartender. Get deep into her background and tell me everything. I want to know if there was any connection between her and the victim, besides what we were told. Anything hidden or that the client might not even be aware of, no matter how trivial."

"Sure, I'll bring you a report later today." Mort took the pages and headed out the door.

A moment later the door opened again and Mort stuck his head back in.

"You neglected to tell me how she was killed. An explosion, wasn't it?"

Melinda laughed. "Geez, don't either of you read the papers? Right you are. Someone blew her up in her car."

Mort nodded.

He turned to leave just as Sarah returned from her lottery ticket run. He grinned widely at her and winked. "Hello beautiful."

She smiled. Mort always made her smile. He was a strange looking man whose arms and legs seemed somehow almost unattached and were disproportionately long compared to the rest of his body. Sarah always thought of R. Crumb's famous Keep on Truckin' Doo-Dah Man whenever she saw him.

He opened the door wider, allowing her to pass, and bowed theatrically before exiting.

Sarah dumped the contents of a small paper bag onto David's desk. "Here you are. Compliments of New York State."

Lowell scooped up a handful and shuffled through each one as if they were playing cards. They were colorful and quite eye-catching, each very different. Win for Life, Lucky Sevens, Manhattan Millionaires, and on and on.

"So how do these things work?" he asked.

"Are you kidding?" asked Sarah. "You've never played one of these?"

"Good God, no."

"You take a coin and scratch off these boxes, like this, and try to match the numbers to the winning numbers."

"On this one," she picked up another, "you try to get three sevens in a row, like tick-tac-toe."

"Marvelous. Let's play."

The three sat in a circle around the coffee table and each took a pile of tickets.

"They really are messy, aren't they?" Lowell began to make little piles of scratch-off stuff. "Put the shavings on this plate."

He pushed a small candy dish into the middle of his desk.

For almost half an hour they scratched off the tickets. Some cost one dollar, some two, five, ten, and even twenty dollars. If someone had a winner they announced it and put it in a separate pile. When they were done Lowell picked up the winners and counted.

"Thirty-eight dollars," he announced, "from two hundred dollars worth of tickets. Is that common?" he asked Sarah.

"I don't know, but it's not the kind of game real gamblers like to play."

Lowell turned to the computer and went to the New York State Lottery website. He hit *scratch-offs* and then *odds of winning.*

"Well, this can't be right," he said, after scrolling through the website.

"What is it?" asked Melinda.

"These odds, they can't be right. How could they get away with this?"

"What's the problem?"

"Well, for example. The odds against winning fifty dollars on a two-dollar ticket are 5,040 to one. How can that be?"

He scrolled down a bit more.

"Here's one where the odds against winning one hundred dollars are 12,600 to one. And a five-hundred-dollar winner on this five-dollar Win for Life is 50,000 to one. If it was an even-money bet it would pay two hundred and fifty thousand dollars. Instead it pays five hundred. My God, with odds like that, you can't even call this gambling."

"What would you call it?" asked his daughter.

"Theft."

Chapter Five

Lowell and Melinda left his office together and said their goodbyes on the corner.

Melinda pulled back the sleeve of her coat. "Good God, it's almost noon. I have to scoot, Dad. Other cases and clients."

Lowell watched as his daughter stuck her hand in the air hoping for an empty cab, often a rare breed in midtown midday. "I'm going to begin my investigation. If you're free we can catch up tonight."

She snagged a cab quickly and got in. "I can meet you at the townhouse at seven." It sped away before he could respond.

As he watched the yellow car carrying his daughter recede downtown he felt a mixture of pride and loss.

Andy was waiting around the corner by the limousine. At six-feet-three, he was an imposing figure, but it was his attention to detail and dry sense of humor that had really been just as important. With a fourth-degree black belt in aikido, Lowell was quite capable of taking care of himself, but it was good to have back-up, and one so pleasant.

Andy held the door as Lowell got in the back.

The first stop was the precinct on East Nineteenth St. His work had led him to this building many times before, and he was familiar with several of the officers, including the sergeant on duty. Lowell always smiled at the looser feeling of a real precinct house, versus the tense and shadowy versions depicted on most TV shows. Just as the public has been trained by CSI to think that lab work was instantaneous, most people never got to see the cordial nature of most precinct desks.

"Good afternoon, Sergeant Miller."

"Mr. Lowell, how are you?" The sergeant looked up from the *Daily News*.

"Quite well."

"Hey, I wanted to thank you for the work you did for my kid last year. After all the psychologists and social workers failed, I don't know how you did it, but he's been doing much better in school and his attitude is remarkable."

"Simply a matter of identifying what is best for the individual," replied Lowell. "Your son's chart showed that he is a night owl, always will be. If you let him make his own hours he will get his work done. Never push a round peg into a square hole."

"Right, right. Thank you again."

"Sergeant, who's in charge of the Winston case?"

"That would be Lieutenant Roland. You working on that?"

"Yes."

"Well, good luck."

◇◇◇

The lieutenant was sitting at his desk when Lowell entered. There were piles of papers, files, and assorted knick-knacks covering the entire top. On the wall behind his desk were framed pictures of Ronald Reagan and George H. Bush. He looked up as Lowell approached.

"Oh, swell, if it isn't the last of the red-hot liberals. This'll just make my day."

"Hello, lieutenant. How have you been?"

"Do you really care?" asked the policeman. "My feet hurt, my daughter's dating a transvestite, I'm eight months behind in my case load, I think my wife's having an affair, I owe the I.R.S. eleven grand and my prostate's the size of a cantaloupe. Glad you asked?"

Lowell sat in the wood guest's chair and looked up at the pictures. "No George W.?"

"I'm a Republican, not an imbecile. To what do I owe the honor of this visit?"

"I'm working on the Winston case."

"Winston? Why?"

He reached over, picked up a file from the top of one of the stacks and opened it. "Judge Farrah Winston, killed, blah, blah, blah. Oh, here it is, attorney Melinda Lowell?" He raised his eyebrows.

Lowell smiled. "My daughter."

Roland shook his head. "Life isn't fair."

"I suppose not."

"So what do you want?"

"First of all, I want access to the victim's apartment. I'm sure your people have been there already, so I won't be interfering with your investigation."

"I suppose that can be arranged. Anything else?"

"I would appreciate it if you could keep me in the loop and let me know any new information that comes across your desk."

Roland shook his head and laughed. "I'll do all your work and you'll take the credit, is that how it is?"

"Lieutenant, all I'm interested in is helping my daughter, and by proxy, her client. You can have all the credit. I would be happy to keep my name out of this whole mess. I abhor publicity."

Roland held up his hand. "Where have I heard that before? All right, I guess I have no choice, anyway. You are a licensed PI working for a reputable defense lawyer. You're by law entitled to see the evidence. But I'm afraid you and your daughter are going to be disappointed."

"Oh?"

"Her client did it all right, and I don't think the D.A. will have a hard time proving it."

"What do you have so far?"

"You know that the judge was killed with a car bomb in the parking garage of the courthouse?"

"Yes, I've seen the preliminary report. The security cameras in the garage showed nothing unusual?"

"Nobody came in or went out all day that couldn't be easily accounted for. And there was nobody else in the garage when she got in her car except her."

"That only leaves two possibilities," said Lowell. "That someone in the building planted it…"

"Or?"

"Or that the bomb was already in place when she came to work in the morning."

"That's what we think."

"So why Johnny Colbert?"

Lowell had crossed paths with the lieutenant on several celebrated cases, most of which had ended with the policeman a frustrating few steps behind his as he solved it. Now he saw that Lieutenant Roland was enjoying himself very much indeed.

The policeman began counting on his fingers. "She had motive: the judge had put her in jail on a contempt charge. She has the temperament. You've met her, right? I've felt safer in lockup with a dozen gang-bangers than I did sitting next to her."

Lowell nodded unconsciously.

"And she had opportunity."

"What opportunity are you talking about?"

The lieutenant smiled. "I see you haven't done your homework yet."

Lowell frowned.

"Didn't you know," continued the cop, "that Johnny Colbert is in the Army Reserves? Or that her specialty happens to be demolition?"

"No, I was not privy to that information. Thank you for that elucidation."

"Privy to that… elucidation," said Roland. "Why don't you talk like normal people?"

"My father was from London."

"So why don't you talk that way all the time?"

"My mother was from Brooklyn."

The lieutenant stood up and walked to the coffee machine. "Want some?" he asked, as he poured himself a cup.

"No thanks, never after noon."

"Not a bad rule. I should try that; I think it's keeping me up at night." Roland took a sip and grimaced. "You're not missing much anyway."

Roland came back and sat on the edge of his desk. "I've got nineteen unsolved murders in my open files. This isn't one of them. According to her squad leader, your sweet little Joanna Colbert is, if you'll excuse the expression, dynamite with explosives. She has the highest rating the army gives. I don't think she would have had any trouble rigging a bomb with a timer or remote control. And, she recently spent two weeks in training where she had access to explosives of various sorts. We're waiting for her C.O. to complete an inventory to see if anything is missing. The D.A. will have a search warrant for her place this afternoon. We'll find what we need."

"Are you looking into any other possible suspects?"

"No. The facts all point toward the defendant and we're satisfied that we have the right person."

Lowell sat silently.

"Something you don't like about this?"

"There's a lot I don't like about it. It's too neat. Too easy."

"Sometimes it works out that way. Not everything is complicated."

"Yes, it is," replied the astrologer, "when human beings are involved."

Roland took that in. "What doesn't work for you?"

"For one thing, as you said, nobody was in the garage with the judge. And a timing device would be very risky. How could my client be sure the victim would go to her car exactly at that time? The judge would likely leave at slightly different times every day, even if she was a creature of habit, which my investigation will tell us."

"Maybe your client just got lucky," said Roland. "She set it to go off at a time when the judge would most likely leave."

"It seems awfully risky to me. No, I don't think a timing device was used. It had to be a remote control. Which means the bomber had to be nearby at the time."

"So, she was across the street watching and set it off by hand. She has the skills to do it, and no alibi."

"Hmm, I suppose it's possible. Aren't there surveillance cameras around the courthouse?"

"A few, but not as many as we'd like. We're looking through the tapes now, but we'd have to be awfully lucky to catch her on camera."

"What did the lab guys come up with?"

"They're still working on it. So far they found pieces of the device rigged to the seat. They're still putting it together. It'll take another few days before they can tell us positively exactly how it was detonated. It was a lot of explosives though."

"Plastic explosives of some sort?"

Roland nodded. "They're trying to track the manufacturer. They think it's made by a French company that deals with U.S. government contracts. Probably something that your client could have come in contact with in the reserves." Roland remained seated. "She had motive, temperament, and opportunity," he said. "And she doesn't have a verifiable alibi. She did it, all right."

"We'll see," said Lowell. "We'll see."

Chapter Six

Andy was waiting when Lowell left the precinct.

"Where to next, boss?"

"It's past two already. This day is slipping by. The victim's home is the closest on my list."

The judge's apartment was on East Forty-eighth Street, a sixth-floor, two-bedroom condo. Lowell looked up at the wall of glass as he got out of the car. The building was brand-new, part of the great apartment building mania that had taken place all over New York City. Hundred-year-old but perfectly solid three- and four-story buildings with vibrant small businesses occupying the ground floors had been knocked down for glass and chrome monstrosities, with interchangeable drug chains swallowing up the retail spaces. How much chrome and aspirin did one city need, Lowell thought.

In fact, the lobby was still being completed, and workmen scurried past him in a comical ballet of near-catastrophes reminiscent of the silent screen. One swung a bucket of white paint barely an inch from Lowell's head as he approached the concierge's desk. Behind it stood a man in his forties dressed in a blue suit with the building's logo stenciled on his lapel.

Lowell presented his card.

The man looked at it for a moment. "Yes, Mr. Lowell, a Lieutenant Roland called. You are expected. Please take either of the first two elevators to the sixth floor, and someone will meet you as you get off."

The elevator was mirrored on all sides, including the ceiling. It was empty and the ride took less than twenty seconds. As he got off his ears popped uncomfortably.

What's the damn hurry? he thought.

"Mr. Lowell?" asked a short, dark-haired man of indeterminate age and ethnic background. He, too, was dressed in the company's standard blue suit and logo.

Lowell nodded.

"The apartment is down this way."

He headed down the hall and turned right, Lowell at his heels. At the second door he stopped, put a key in the lock, and opened the door.

"I was told to give you free rein, so just lock up and bring the keys back to the front desk when you're done."

He handed Lowell the keys and left.

Lowell took out the astrological birth chart of Judge Farrah Winston and looked around her apartment to see if things jelled. It was a habit he had gotten into years before. If something was very amiss and didn't concur with the chart, he would notice immediately. But that wasn't the case here. Lowell looked at the natal chart. She was a Virgo with the Moon and Venus also in that most concise and detail-oriented sign, a difficult placement for the planets of love. She was probably quite critical of her suitors and could be very demanding. But the apartment also showed her conscientious nature and attention to specifics common with those planetary placements.

She was obviously a painstakingly meticulous woman. Everything was in its place. The carpet was off-white, a challenging choice for a neat-freak. The furniture was expensive, but not pretentious in any way. The living room had an airy feel about it. Nothing was too cluttered.

One of the bedrooms had been converted into an office. There was a desk next to a window that caught a slight view of the East River. Lowell smiled to himself at the fact that the East River wasn't really a river at all. It was a several-mile-long strait connecting Upper New York Bay to the Long Island Sound.

The tides made the water move like a river. But New Yorkers' minds are hard to change once they are locked in on something. So a river it is.

Uranus was very active in Judge Winston's chart at the time of her death, which one would expect with such a sudden and violent act. That planet also holds domain over all things electronic, and he knew where he would find some of the answers he sought. He turned on the computer but couldn't get past the password.

Damn, he thought, *why didn't I bring Mort?*

The bedroom told him little. There was a king-sized bed, a matching dresser and night table, several lamps, and a large chair, almost big enough to be considered a day bed, all brand-new. Her closets were well organized and her clothes, though expensive, as the designer labels attested, were neither flamboyant nor showy. Most of her possessions spoke of a conservative individual who took pride in her appearance.

He did the usual movie-detective search, looking behind paintings, pulling out drawers, and searching for the hidden safe-deposit key. He wondered if anyone ever really found a clue that way, or if it was just an easy plot device for Hollywood writers.

Still, despite all its sense of normalcy, there was something amiss in that apartment. It took a few moments to put his finger on it. It wasn't what he saw that bothered him so much as what he didn't see. Everything was in its place, but where was anything personal? There were no family pictures or bundles of old letters. It was almost as if this were just a stop-off, a pied-à-terre. If the judge had planned on staying in this building, wouldn't she have brought her most precious possessions?

Lowell left the keys with the concierge and went out past the workers as they attempted to finish the lobby.

He walked out of the building. It was a bright sunny afternoon with just a slight chill. He looked at his watch. It was almost four and too late to get much more done for the case. Andy stood next to the limo, ever patient. He opened the back door.

"How'd it go, boss?"

"Okay, I guess. There really wasn't much there."

"What's the next stop?"

"Andy, I'd like to walk a few blocks. I'll be okay. Just stay near."

Lowell had always enjoyed walking through the city, and he was now forced to limit them, and always to pre-sunrise sojourns.

He had made a point of seeking out the unusual side streets, the quiet corners, the places of history, but lately Manhattan had lost much of its bohemian, circus-like charm. More and more people dressed and looked the same. All the stores were the same. All the buildings were the same. One neighborhood was virtually indistinguishable from another. All the new buildings were modern ugly.

But he still liked looking at people. What was it the client had called it? Something about swimming, no, surfing, face surfing, that was it. The more he thought about the concept, the more it made him smile. He started looking at the people he passed, brushing each with just a glance. It was like riding waves, something he'd enjoyed immensely in his youth in Long Beach, Long Island, where his grandmother had a summer home. He bounced off one mug and onto another, careful not to stay too long. You could washout, a glance is acceptable, a leer is not. *Face surfing*: he'd have to remember that.

A homeless man sat against a wall, holding out a cup. David knew giving him money was like throwing a toothpick to a drowning man, but he fished a few bucks out of his pocket nonetheless. He couldn't turn a blind eye to someone in need.

The man nodded and mumbled, but didn't look up.

As Lowell walked on, he passed several stores with dusty For Rent signs in the window. He remembered the last recession, back in the eighties. It wasn't a pleasant memory. And this one promised to be deeper and much longer. There were more people living on the streets than there had been only a year before. When the landlord-friendly rezoning laws took effect, they wiped out the majority of affordable housing. But, like some bizarre apocalyptic weapon, it took away the buildings but left the people behind.

He stopped into a newspaper store and there they were: spools of scratch-off tickets in plain sight: dozens of varieties in all kinds of colors and attractive decorations. Why had he never seen them before?

There was a line of people waiting to play the lottery. Did his local store have such a queue? He had always just walked in and left the money for his newspaper. Perhaps there was a line that he hadn't been aware of. That wasn't good news. Was he just not paying attention?

He watched and listened.

"Yes, sir," said the man behind the counter to his next customer. "Numbers?"

The man nodded.

"Go ahead," said the store worker.

"Seven one five, three straight and one boxed," said the man.

The counterman quickly entered the information into the computer, which spit out one ticket after another.

"Three twelve, four straight and one boxed, eight one two, a dollar and a dollar, four three eight, two straight and one boxed, five cash mega, two take five quick picks and give me one of the New York Millions."

When he finished, the next customer ran off her list of numbers.

Lowell was mesmerized. After ten minutes or so he left. Outside he saw a man looking through his tickets.

"Do you mind if I ask you something?"

The man quickly put the pile of tickets into his pocket and looked at Lowell suspiciously. "What do you want?"

"Forgive me for intruding, but I noticed that you played a lot of lottery tickets just now."

"What are you, my mother?"

"No, don't get me wrong." Lowell held up his hand. "I was just trying to understand the appeal, that's all."

The man looked Lowell up and down.

"You don't gamble?" he asked. "No, I guess a guy like you wouldn't have to."

He walked away.

"What are you doing, writing a book?" came a voice behind him.

Lowell turned toward the voice. It emanated from a tall man with graying hair and a jovial face. His collar was a little frayed, but otherwise he was clean-shaven and his hair was neatly combed.

"Something like that."

"What do you want to know? I'll tell you." The man was holding a few lottery tickets.

Lowell was blunt. "Why do you do it?"

"Do what, gamble?"

Lowell nodded. "I'm trying to understand the mentality behind it all. Certainly you must know that the odds against your winning more than a few dollars are astronomical."

The man nodded in agreement.

"So why do you play? You're almost sure to lose."

"But I might win big," he said with a grin.

"You always gambled?"

"As far back as I can remember. When I was a kid my family would hold poker games after every holiday meal."

"Let me tell you something," he continued. "I'm sixty-two now. When I was a younger man I was married to a wonderful woman. She was beautiful and loving and we had a terrific life. Eventually we had a boy, but no matter how much I tried I could never make ends meet. One day, I was twenty-five I think; I bought a lottery ticket and won two hundred thousand dollars. I thought I had died and gone to heaven. We moved out of the dump we were in and Lisa stopped working.

"Anyway, I started getting, I don't know, fidgety or something. I began buying more and more of the damn things until I was spending a hundred a day or more. Then I would go to Atlantic City with my friends, or the race track. I'd win sometimes, but

I lost a lot more often. I would wake up in the middle of the night in sweats thinking about my next game.

"Then one night I got into a poker game. I was in way over my head with pots of thousands of dollars. The game was crooked, but I didn't know that until later. Until it was too late. I lost everything. Lisa, my son, my house, and my job."

He looked close to tears.

"Didn't see my kid for almost twenty years."

Lowell felt for the man, having made his own mistakes in life. But he had to ask.

"But you still gamble?"

"Yes, but now I only spend ten dollars a day, never more. And if I win something it goes into the bank. Maybe this time if I hit big I'll be smarter."

There was an awkward silence. The man looked away squinting, either looking at the past or the future. Lowell cleared his throat and spoke first.

"Thank you for your time, and I wish you all the luck in the world."

"Hey, thanks for listening, and good luck with that book of yours. I hope it helps some others. You need any more insights, I'm always in the neighborhood."

Lowell walked another two or three blocks, passing a tiny news kiosk, a card store and a Korean deli, all advertising lottery games. What had overtaken society? Why this gambling mania? Was life really so chancy, so desperate?

At the next corner he saw Andy next to the limo. He got in.

"I don't have to be at the townhouse until seven. Let's take a drive."

Andy understood what that meant. His boss wanted to be alone to think. He pushed a button on the car door and the partition between the front and back seats went up.

Lowell leaned back and closed his eyes for a moment. What was it about his species that made them so self-destructive? So hell-bent on making and then keeping money. The drive was strong enough to push gambling against all odds, and for some, to kill.

His limousine was an office on wheels. The body and interior were made to specification by Richard Delaney, an inventor and old friend now living in Switzerland. He'd had the body elongated and a complete workplace with a desk, drawers, and computer terminals installed. A built-in swivel chair was bolted to the floor.

Delaney had also invented a new type of plasma screen that would make him rich as soon as the patents became official and the bugs were worked out. He had installed them into the windows of the limo. When turned off they were completely transparent. But when activated they were quite something.

Lowell turned to the elaborate console. He fiddled with one of the knobs, twisting it until it read #15. Then he pushed ON and sat back on the couch. The compartment darkened slightly and the windows began to change. Suddenly he was driving through a rainstorm on the coast of New England. Although he knew it was late afternoon on a sunny day, in the limo it was now late at night and the wind and rain were howling their complaints. He touched the window, and just as he expected it was damp and cool. The rain drops on the roof were steady and yet varied. There were twenty-four mini speakers to help create the atmosphere.

It was a wonderful invention. Some day they would be in restaurants, nightclubs and homes. *Can't get away this weekend? Pop in Ambience and spend it in Tahiti.*

In the meantime there were only a few people Delaney trusted with his invention, and Lowell was proud to be one of them.

He sat back and meditated. The rain helped. Recordings of actual rain storms were looped together in oscillating order. Delaney had never found a computer program that could create the feel of nature. So he relied on the real thing and recorded all of his sounds live, then digitized them so he could manipulate them as needed. But you had to start with the real thing. You can't clone it. The human mind would eventually figure it out and it would become repetitious. This way it was as close to the real deal as possible.

What was Judge Winston doing to get someone mad enough at her to want to blow her up? Could it really be over a debt of a few thousand dollars and a little time in lock up? Time would tell.

He dozed.

He dreamt that he was in the jungle chasing an elusive prey as rain fell like tiny invaders, pelting him in a ceaseless cascade of pesky droplets that turned into scratch-off tickets as they landed on his head. In the dream, he spotted his quarry as it ducked behind a giant tree. He ran to the tree and circled around, just missing his target each time.

Chapter Seven

Andy dropped Lowell off at the townhouse a little before seven.

Lowell punched in the security code on the tall metal gate and entered the front courtyard. The house was set back from the sidewalk about twenty feet, with a metal table and several chairs on the patio, although it was rare that anyone sat there any longer. The house had been designed in another era when New Yorkers were more sociable with their neighbors.

"Hello," he shouted, as he came through the door.

"Mr. Lowell, is that you?" Julia stuck her head out of the kitchen door. "Melinda just called. She's on her way uptown and should be here in a few minutes. Would you like me to fix you a drink?"

"Thanks," he replied. "A beer, please. A Hoegaarden."

He went into the den and turned the TV to CNN. Julia came in with a bottle and chilled Pilsner glass and set them down on the table. She knew that Lowell preferred to pour his own beer, and that he liked it served between 39 and 42 degrees. He had a special mini-fridge put in the kitchen.

"Thank you, Julia. So what dinner surprise have you planned for me?"

"It wouldn't be much of a surprise if I told you, now would it?" Julia headed back to the kitchen.

He poured the beer into the ice cold glass, allowing a head to form about an inch high, the way he liked it. Most people didn't know how to pour beer properly. He took a sip and gave a silent sigh. He liked beer, more than he should.

He heard the front door open.

"Melinda?" he called out.

"Hi, dad, where are you?"

"In the den."

She came in and kissed her father on the cheek. "How was your afternoon?"

"Busy. I went to see Lieutenant Roland. He's in charge of the case. Then I saw the judge's apartment. Tomorrow I'll go to her chambers. I need to speak to her clerk."

"What did you find in her place?"

"Nothing useful. I want to go back again and bring Mort along this time. See if we can get a look at her computer files."

He took a long draw of beer.

"I learned some interesting things about our client while I was with Lieutenant Roland."

"Oh, did you?" Melinda shrugged. "Maybe I'll have a beer too."

She got up and walked into the kitchen, returning a few moments later with a chilled glassful of beer. It had no head. She didn't seem to notice.

"So what do you think about the future of real estate in the city?" she asked, as she sat on the couch.

Lowell looked at her with amusement. "That tactic didn't work when you were a kid and it doesn't work now."

"What do you mean?"

"You hoped I would forget what we were talking about. It only works when I'm very preoccupied."

"I'm sure I don't know what you mean."

"Sure. We were talking about your client and the fact that she is a member of the Army reserve."

"Oh, that. That's nothing at all. I can…"

"Or that her specialty is explosives."

"Oh, that."

"Why didn't you tell me?"

"Because I knew you would react just the way you are. Just because someone can do something doesn't mean he or she necessarily did do it."

Lowell shook his head. "It would have been nice if you had told me."

"Okay, so she's a hard-assed, foul-mouthed woman who rubs people the wrong way."

"Who just happens to have an expertise in the very method used to kill the victim."

"Who just happens to have an expertise in the very method used to kill the victim," repeated Melinda. "But that doesn't mean she did it. If every crude and uncouth human being were put in jail…"

"…this planet might actually be worth living on."

"Oh, dad."

They drank their beer in silence until Julia came in and announced that dinner was ready.

They took their drinks and entered the small alcove next to the kitchen where Julia had set the table and lit two candles.

"Oh, Julia, this is just lovely, thank you," said Melinda.

When they were seated, Julia brought in Melinda's dinner first and placed it in front of her. A rather large sirloin steak, baked potato, and asparagus.

"Steak?" She looked over at her father. "You don't mind?"

"Just because I'm a vegetarian doesn't mean you have to be."

"Yum," she said, as she sliced into the steak. "Perfectly pink."

Julia returned with Lowell's meal and placed it in front of him. He looked down at it and then up at her.

"What is it?"

"It's tofu lasagna with layers of eggplant and soy cheese, all organic. Surprised?"

"I am."

He picked up his fork and took a bite.

"Julia, you have outdone yourself. Bring a little bit for Melinda."

"Oh, no, thanks. I've got more than I can handle here. But you're welcome to a slice of cow, if you'd like."

Then she giggled.

Lowell looked at her and smiled.

"I'm glad you're here."

"Me, too." She reached over and patted his hand. "Me, too."

They each ate a few bites, then Lowell returned to the topic at hand.

"All the evidence points to Johnny. She has a motive, opportunity, and no alibi. This is not the easiest case you've ever had."

"Look, maybe I'm just a foolish idealist."

"Maybe?"

"But I still believe that everyone is entitled to a proper defense. And I'm going to give her the best I can come up with." She sipped her beer. "There is very little left of the American dream for so many people, and it's too easy for the individual to fall into the cracks in this system. All I can do is try to save one at a time. Right now Johnny is the one."

"Despite all the evidence aimed at her, you're still willing to take this on, no matter where it leads?"

"Not despite it," replied Melinda. "Because of it."

Lowell savored a bite of tofu.

"So what are you going to do next?" she finally asked.

"Find out who killed Judge Farrah Winston. Even if it was our client."

"That's not going to be the case." She smiled.

Chapter Eight

Mort's mouth was already working, stoked on two morning coffees, when he entered Lowell's office. Two coffees before nine, two more by noon.

"I can't find any connection between Johnny Colbert and Judge Winston. I've traced their movements back to childhood. As far as I can tell, they've never crossed paths outside the courtroom."

"Tell me what you can about the victim."

He handed Lowell several photographs showing a stunningly beautiful woman with long chestnut-brown hair.

"This is her?"

Mort nodded. "She wasn't just a pretty package. She graduated summa cum laude from Columbia Law, winning all sorts of awards and accolades. She's originally from Utah, although her family is not Mormon."

"So how did she wind up in debt court?"

"That's a good question." Mort glanced at his notebook. "Right after graduation she was grabbed by Coleman, Weiss, and Barton, one of the most prestigious firms in Westchester. She quickly became known as the Golden Girl, able to hook big clients on any side of a legal question. And of course with big clients came big fees."

"And she gave all that up just to preside over this court of cases better heard by Judge Judy?"

Mort shrugged in a comical fashion. His exceedingly long limbs seemed to flap like wings.

"I know, I don't get it either. She took the job a few years ago."

"Well," said Lowell, "I guess that's a good place to start. I want you to follow her career from the time she got out of law school. Find out why a talented, intelligent, and attractive lawyer would give up a thriving career in private practice for the lowest rung on the ladder."

"I'll see what I can come up with."

Lowell picked up Johnny's chart.

"This week's full moon eclipse is exactly in square to our client's moon, and I'm worried that there might be an incident."

"Trouble on Riker's Island? Don't be silly." Mort laughed, the sound an odd squawk.

"I may have no choice but to put up bail for her."

"You'll make Melinda happy, anyway."

Lowell sighed. "That's true. I'll look into it later. Right now I'm going down to the judge's chambers to talk to her clerk. Then at some point I want to go back to her apartment. I want you with me so you can use that bizarre brain of yours to get into her home computer."

Lowell stood up, shrugged on his favorite leather jacket, and rearranged his ponytail on top of the collar.

Andy drove Lowell downtown to the courthouse. It was ten and the place was already a madhouse. He went up to the judge's chambers on the third floor where he was met by her clerk, Larry Rosen.

"I was Judge Winston's clerk for the past three years," he told Lowell, on the way to his office. "I've never met a nicer or more capable person in the whole system. It's really a damn shame."

He waved his hand around the corridor at the people they were passing. "We all miss her."

"What was she like?"

Rosen smiled, gesturing Lowell into his small office outside the judge's chambers. "She was an exceedingly competent jurist with a clear and sharp mind. She never used her looks nor let them get in her way."

"So how did she wind up here?"

Rosen moved around to his side of the desk as Lowell sat.

"As in any career there are stepping stones."

"So she was planning a career move?"

"I'm not really at liberty to discuss the judge's plans."

"Were you here when it happened?"

"I've already told all of this to the police."

"I know, but if you don't mind, it's better to get things from the source than to try and interpret what each person has added to the story."

"All right," Rosen let out an exasperated sigh. "I was working at my desk out front when I heard the explosion."

"How long before that had Judge Winston left?"

"About ten minutes, maybe fifteen, no more."

"How do you know that so specifically?"

"Because I always wait fifteen minutes exactly after she leaves before I go home for the night, in case she forgot something. It's like a ritual with us. Or at least it was."

His face showed just the appropriate amount of grief. But Lowell came from a family of actors and knew full well that we all wear many masks. There was only one place he could always find the truth about someone. In their birth chart.

"Did she leave at exactly the same time each night?"

"The judge didn't believe in absolute rigidity. She always wanted some variation, even if it was in the small details. So, no, she made it a point not to arrive at exactly eight, or to leave at exactly five. It could be as much as a half-hour in either direction."

Lowell nodded. She was a New Moon baby. They like to be the initiators, the lead dog. Not sheep.

"Did you get along with the judge?"

"I thought she was a wonderfully intelligent and charming woman. She made clerking more fun."

"And you two never had problems?"

"Problems? Not at all. She and I saw eye to eye on almost everything. Especially politically."

"Why was that?"

"We are, were, both conservative Republicans. But we came to it from different angles."

"What do you mean?"

"I was raised by sixties liberals. My father was a New York Democrat assemblyman who fought hard for the issues he believed in. I never shared his political point of view. When I decided to go into law he felt sure I would turn out to be the same liberal voice he had been. But he was wrong. In fact, he was wrong about almost everything." Rosen reached for a deli take-out cup of coffee and swirled it in his hand. "Judge Winston came from a staunch Roosevelt-hating Republican family from out West. And she approved of their politics. She thought I was smart, and she needed someone who had the same values she held. So I became her clerk."

"She ever piss you off?"

"Sometimes. Of course."

"But I thought you two saw eye to eye on everything?"

"Oh, there are always a few little disagreements. I mean, my God, nobody gets along a hundred percent of the time. But never anything beyond a minor intellectual debate."

"Were you present when my client was in Judge Winston's courtroom two days before the murder?"

"I was, in fact. I had brought some papers down to the judge and witnessed the altercation between the two."

"And had you seen the defendant previously?"

"Yes, she had been in Judge Winston's court a number of times."

"I see. So she was quite aware of the victim?"

"Oh yes, they had words in the past, although not as boisterous as on that day."

"What was the judge's reaction to Ms. Colbert's outburst?"

"She was as mad as I had ever seen her. For the rest of the day it bothered her."

"Did she feel threatened by the defendant?"

"Well, she must have. After she had her released from lockup she asked me to walk her to her car that night."

"And that was unusual?"

"She had never before asked for an escort. Judge Winston was a very self-sufficient person. She never asked anyone for help. But after she released the defendant, she must have felt some fear."

"But only two days later, the day of the murder, she didn't request that you accompany her?"

"No, I guess she felt the threat had passed."

Rosen raised his right hand to his forehead. "If only I had, maybe I could have done something."

"Did Judge Winston have any enemies that you knew of?"

"She was the sweetest, brightest person I had ever worked with. Everybody loved her."

"Nobody had ever threatened her, as far as you know?"

"No."

"But if she was afraid for her life, as you implied, why would she release Ms. Colbert? Wouldn't she have exhausted every possible means of keeping her in custody and protecting herself?"

"Judge Winston was very strong and independent. She didn't let things get to her the way they do to most people. I think she just wanted the whole incident to go away. If anything, she was probably just afraid that your client might attack her in the garage, not put a bomb in her car."

"So her fear was rather fleeting, is that it?"

"I don't think she ever thought in terms of vengeance or underhanded acts. Farrah Winston was a direct and honest person who looked the world in the face and expected others to do the same. She was genuinely shocked when a friend or associate bad-mouthed her or acted in a dishonest way. She figured if that woman was going to hurt her, she would do it face to face."

"Okay, thanks for your time."

He got up, and his hand was on the doorknob when he turned suddenly.

"Oh, would you mind telling me your birth date?"

"Why, of course not," Rosen said. "April 17, 1968."

Lowell took out a small notebook out and made a notation. Then he returned it to his jacket pocket.

"I'll be in touch."

The next stop was uptown, the law offices of Bernstein and Milford. It was just before noon as he arrived. Andy had navigated traffic up Park like a slalom skier.

Lowell was quickly ushered into the private suite of this prestigious firm's senior partner.

"Won't you sit down?" Mark Milford was a good four or five inches taller than Lowell, in his early fifties, with sandy hair just starting to grey.

The office was huge, a corner suite with floor-to-ceiling windows overlooking Park Avenue. It was a beautiful room furnished in modern metallic, with a four-stool wet bar, couches and lavishly embroidered rugs, all presumably marked up an absurd amount by a corporate decorator. After some consideration and a battle between envy and pride, Lowell decided he preferred his own office. It was homier.

"Would you like something? Some coffee perhaps? Or something stronger?"

"No," said Lowell, "nothing. I won't take up too much of your time. There were just a few questions."

"Of course, anything I can do to help."

"You were on the phone from here with Judge Winston when the explosion took place?"

"That's right."

"How long were you and Ms. Winston dating?"

"We met about a month ago at a dinner. We were each getting over a bad breakup and just kind of fell into each other's lives. I feel cheated by her death. We were only just starting to feel comfortable with each other when it happened."

"I'm sorry for your loss. The judge was getting over a breakup? With whom?"

"She never told me his name, and I never asked. But I had the impression it was someone important, and probably a bit older than she. Well, of course, so am I."

"So you have no idea who this person is?"

"I did come in once when she was on the phone, and I'm sure it was with him. But I never did find out his name." The lawyer paused. "I understand that you are an astrologer."

"At the moment I am working in the capacity of a licensed private investigator for whom astrology is a tool, yes."

"Well, that must be a fascinating business. You must read my cards someday. Perhaps we can hire you for our Christmas party. People love that kind of stuff."

Lowell smiled just a little.

"What do you charge?"

"A million dollars."

"Huh?"

"Plus carfare."

"Oh, I see; a joke. Good one. I beg your pardon. Sometimes I speak without thinking."

"No problem."

"What else can I tell you about Farrah?"

"I understand she has a sister."

"That's right," said Milford, "lives somewhere in Jersey. I only met her once. She's nothing like Farrah. Almost the complete opposite in every way."

"Did they get along?"

"You know how it is with siblings. They were nice enough to each other, but I felt a little underlying conflict. Maybe some envy."

"What was Farrah's mood like during the past few weeks? Was she tense, or apprehensive in any way?"

Milford got up, walked over to the bar, and poured himself a glass of juice. Even in his simplest actions there was an air of self-importance.

"Not that I noticed. But she had been quite busy recently and I didn't see that much of her. Also, she was very excited about something, but she never had a chance to tell me what. In fact, she was on her way to pick me up for dinner to discuss it when she was killed."

"You have no idea what she was going to tell you?"

"None. Although I knew that it was very important for her. And it was most certainly related to her career."

"Why do you say that?"

"Because the only things that ever excited Farrah had to do with her career. She was a very ambitious woman with big ideas and an overwhelming potential. I know something big had been in the works for some months. In fact, she was already involved in it when we met. Whatever it was, it would have made her very happy."

"But you have no idea what it was?"

"Sorry, I wish I could be of more help."

"I understand. Would you mind giving me your date, time and place of birth?"

"Of course not. It's a matter of record anyway. I was born on June 14, 1956, in New London, Connecticut. I believe the time was 7:15 a.m."

"Thank you. Just one more question. Do you know of anyone who would want her dead?"

"Farrah was a wonderful woman," said Milford. "She was bright and energetic, and always willing to talk about anything. I really don't think she had an enemy in the world."

"Well," said Lowell, "she had one."

Chapter Nine

The woman lit her third cigarette in the ten minutes Lowell had been there. She blew the smoke out of the right side of her mouth trying not to direct it toward him, but in so small a room it was virtually impossible for him not to share.

Sarah had retrieved the address in New Jersey and Andy had easily found it on his Garmin. The string of lights inside the Lincoln Tunnel played across the monitor screen inside the limo as Lowell entered the clerk's and lawyer's birth information. He'd processed the two interviews, but now it was time to get another perspective. The city's skyline looked like a row of jagged teeth, but that vertical image gave way to the flatness of the Jersey's meadowlands, which still contained a few patches of actual meadow.

"You know how they always say one sister gets the looks, the other gets the brains?" Her voice was tiny. "Well, look at me. I got short-changed twice."

She was a mousy little woman who looked at the floor when she spoke. She seemed pathologically shy and made Lowell feel a little uncomfortable. She nervously flicked the cigarette into the ashtray even when no ash had accumulated.

"Even as a baby Farrah was beautiful. I think my parents knew she would grow up to be gorgeous when they decided to name her after a movie star. Farrah always had her poster up in our room when we were kids. I hated it."

She inhaled about half the cigarette in one drag.

"She was the beautiful one, so my parents figured I was the one with the smarts, and they pushed me and pushed me. When I didn't get A's they sent me to tutors, therapists, motivational training, anything one of their friends sent their kid to. But it didn't help. I'm just not that smart. But Farrah was. She started getting straight A's in elementary school and never stopped. You know, in high school she was both the valedictorian and prom queen. Can you imagine? Never in the history of our school had that happened. And I was her sister. Her ugly, untalented, dumb sister. Just about anyone who became my friend only wanted to get close to her."

"You were older?"

"Yes, by three years."

Lowell had to sit forward in his chair to hear her. "So why did you move east?

"What was I supposed to do? She was the magnet, the one who brought the boys. All our lives I got the leftovers, not that I cared, mind you. If it wasn't for her, I never would have had the courage to talk to a boy, let alone kiss one. When Farrah graduated from Columbia and decided to stay in New York, I moved here, too."

There were pictures of her with her husband and child on the side table next to the couch.

"You have a lovely family."

"Thank you, I got lucky. I managed to hook a nice guy. But I only met him because Farrah had a date one night and had to fix the guy's cousin up with someone or else he would have had to cancel."

Lowell glanced at the pile of bills on the coffee table between them, and she noticed.

"We were doing fine until my husband got laid off."

"I'm sorry to hear that."

"We'll survive."

Lowell wanted to get to the present day. "Can you think of anyone who would want to hurt your sister?"

She continued to look at the floor as she spoke, holding the lit cigarette in front of her face, seemingly unaware of the curl of smoke invading her eyes.

"I've been trying to figure that out since this happened. She was so popular, it couldn't be someone who hated her. Nobody did. So I figure it was someone who loved her."

"You mean someone who was jealous of her?"

"I know what you're getting at. I wasn't jealous of my sister. I loved her. Sure, I wish I had her looks or her personality, but I did all right. Maybe Joey isn't the best-looking guy on the block, but he loves me and he tries to make a good home. I think it was one of her boyfriends."

"Anyone in particular?"

"Nah, she didn't always tell me who she was dating. But when you look like her you can be sure there will be jealousy. The last one I met was some lawyer named Milford."

"Do you know who she was dating before Mark Milford?"

She shook her head. "She kept that one a secret. I always wondered who she was with, but whenever I asked her she would just laugh and say that it was post-graduate work, whatever that meant."

"Do you know if there was an insurance policy?"

She picked her head up and looked Lowell in the eye.

"Yes, there was," she said, her voice a bit louder, "for three hundred thousand dollars. And before you bother asking, yes, I am the beneficiary. And except for a little she left to our parents, I am also the main beneficiary of her will."

This time she blew the smoke directly into Lowell's face.

"Was there anything else?"

Chapter Ten

Andy had picked up sandwiches for the ride back, and they were just entering in the maw of midtown when Lowell's phone rang. He was enjoying the simulation of a bright sunny day in southern California by the coast highway, and the sudden interruption jarred him back to reality.

"Dad, it's me," said his daughter, in her professional voice. "There's been an incident on Riker's Island. Someone stabbed Johnny and I'm on my way to see her."

"How badly is she hurt?" *Damn, just on the full moon. I should have acted on my instincts.*

"I don't know much. I'll call you when I know more."

After they'd hung up. Lowell picked up the phone and made a call. He got to the office about twenty minutes later.

"Hello, Sarah."

"You had about a zillion calls."

"Could you be just a little more precise in the number?"

"Twenty-six." She handed him a stack of little slips.

Lowell entered his office and shut the door. He looked through the messages, returned the calls he thought necessary and did further work on the charts of the principals in the case.

An hour later the intercom buzzed.

"Melinda is on line one."

He picked up the phone. "Where are you?"

"I'm at the hospital. Johnny's going to be okay, they just stabbed her in the shoulder."

"Still scary, if not as bad as it could've been. I'm relieved."

"They told me you'd arranged bail. Thank you so much."

"You're welcome."

"When we're done processing her release we'll come by the office. Johnny wants to thank you personally."

"That's not really necessary."

"We'll be there later," said Melinda, firmly.

"You sounded exactly like your mother just now, you know that?"

Melinda was silent.

He sighed. "Let me know when you're on the way and I'll be sure to be here."

"Thank you."

He went back to work. The judge's chart was a study in contradictions. Here was a woman with a brilliant and critical mind, capable of catching the details in things while still able to grasp the bigger picture. She had been self-assured and had had a commanding presence. Yet with Mars in Libra in trine to Jupiter her ego wasn't really strong as much as very present. It was conjunct Mercury so she was able to direct it through her speech and other communications. She could be very persuasive, yet could herself be coerced by people of great power or magnetism if they asserted their egos. With Jupiter, ruler of the law, in the 10th House of vocation in her natal chart, her career in the legal profession held immense promise. That, in trine to the Mars – Mercury conjunct, gave her charisma and a sharp mind. With Uranus in Judge Winston's 3rd House, her sister would be nervous and a little unusual. Their relationship was erratic and at times possibly explosive. The chart also showed that the judge had great ambition and would have been able to make the big things happen. And her chart looked as though she was just about to. The future had been very promising for Farrah Winston. Mark Milford was right. Whatever she was about to tell him was very important indeed.

◇◇◇

Melinda entered the office with their client. Johnny's right arm was in a sling and bandaged across the shoulder.

"I want to thank you for bailing me out," she said, "I don't think I would have lasted much longer in there."

"Sit down over there on the couch and tell me what happened," said Lowell.

Johnny sat on the couch too fast and accidentally banged her elbow on the arm rest. She grimaced, but didn't utter a sound.

"There were three of them," Johnny began, "tough bitches. They might have been a gang, I'm not sure. They're not allowed to wear colors on Riker's. Anyway, they cornered me in the corridor and one said, '*This is for the judge*', and then stuck the knife in me. I kicked one of them and ran with the damn thing still sticking out of my shoulder. I collapsed near my cell and a couple of guards took me to the infirmary. I think they would have just left me, but too many people had seen me lying there. The whole thing felt like a set-up."

"What do you mean?"

"I was sent down that corridor by a guard. It's usually patrolled on a regular basis and there are at least one or two guards in the area. Today there were none."

"What happened to the inmates who attacked you?"

"Nothing. Nobody's willing to say anything. Do you blame them?"

"I've filed a request for a formal investigation," said Melinda. "But so far I've been stonewalled."

"You're not gonna get anywhere with this," said Johnny. "Someone paid them to slice me up, and whoever that was has a lot of clout. I think the guards were in on it and they were supposed to kill me."

Lowell nodded. "I'm afraid you may be right," he said, "which is why I bailed you out. You won't be safe until this trial is over."

"And then what? How long do you think I'll last in prison if they convict me?"

"Well," said Lowell, "we'll just have to make sure they don't."

"Johnny," said Melinda, "would you mind waiting outside for a minute? I need to talk to my father."

Lowell buzzed Sarah. A moment later she opened the door.

"Yes, boss?"

"Would you please take our client into the conference room and get her some refreshments?"

"Be glad to." Sarah turned to Johnny. "We weren't formally introduced. I'm Sarah."

"Johnny."

"Well, come on. Would you like some coffee?"

"You got any beer?"

Sarah closed the door behind them, with a quick look of amusement at Lowell.

"What am I going to do with her?" said Melinda.

"Why must you do anything with her?"

"I don't think this was a gang hit, do you?"

"No."

"I mean, why would a street gang give a damn one way or another if a judge gets whacked?"

"They wouldn't," said Lowell. "They would most likely be glad. Unless they were paid to give a damn."

"And if she's right and some guards were in on it, she wouldn't last a day in prison."

"Probably not."

"And if the hit was ordered from the outside," said Melinda, "that means she can't go back to her place or she could be in danger."

"I suppose."

"Exactly. So you see my point."

"Uh, what point is that?"

"That Johnny has to stay at your townhouse until the trial is over."

"Oh, no."

"But daddy…"

"Daddy?"

"But let me explain. If someone is out to get her she can't go home and…"

"No."

"But…"

"No."

"You're such a jerk sometimes."

"I know. But it's still no."

Chapter Eleven

"Would you like some more lemonade?" asked Julia.

"No, thank you, but it's really very good. Not too sweet."

"I make it myself," said the housekeeper, unable to keep the pride from her voice. "I don't like the package stuff."

"Me, either," said Johnny.

"Let me know if you need anything."

She went back into the house, leaving Johnny lying on one of the lounge chairs in the backyard. It was unseasonably warm for November, and she grabbed for what little sun she could find. Lowell had bailed her out only the day before, but already her jail pallor had improved. Her shoulder was still bandaged, but she didn't need the sling. It lay on the ground next to her, along with her shirt. Her white bra was in stark contrast to the orange-and-green tattoo of a lion across her chest. She unhooked her top to take advantage of the warmth of the last of the autumn sun's rays reflecting off a distant high-rise.

She was half napping when the door from the house opened with a squeak.

Johnny woke to see both Lowells staring at her. "Hey, how are you guys?"

"Would you please put some clothes on," said the astrologer.

"Huh?" She looked down. "Oh, yeah, I forgot. Hey, don't let it bother you. I don't mind."

"Well, I do," he said.

"Yeah, okay. Don't have a fit. But they're nice, huh?" She cupped her breasts in her hands and presented them to David like a plate of ripe fruit. The lion tattoo covered her entire chest, with the right nipple as the nose of the beast and an orange mane streaking around the bosom.

"Yes, they're very nice. Now put something on."

Melinda watched this exchange with great amusement. She wasn't sure, but she thought her father was blushing.

Johnny put her top back on and gingerly pulled her shirt around her shoulders.

"That better?"

"Thank you," said Lowell. He came and sat at the backyard table. "Have you ever had your astrology chart done?"

"No. What's it like?"

"So you don't know anything about your chart?"

"Just that I'm Aquarius, right?"

"And nobody ever told you anything else, like where your moon is, or your rising sign?"

She shook her head. "I had my aura read once by some woman came into the bar."

"You see how powerful the ascendant is," said Lowell, turning to Melinda. "The rising sign represents the physical body and the projection of the self-image. She has a Leo rising sign and unconsciously has herself tattooed with a rather prominent image of a lion."

"I've always been drawn to lions. When I was a kid I used to wear my hair long and comb it up like a mane."

"Wonderful, just a marvelous example. I must remember to put this in my next lecture."

He went on, "Tell me again exactly what these women said when they attacked you."

"I told you yesterday."

Lowell didn't like Johnny. He found her rude, obnoxious, and inappropriately aggressive. And he certainly wasn't happy that she was staying at his house. But he loved his daughter, so he bit his lip.

"Well, tell me again."

"The big one said: '*This is for the judge.*' Then she stuck the blade into my shoulder. I think she was aiming for my heart, but I turned away just in time."

"Is that all she said?"

"Well, when I got away and was running down the corridor I heard one of them say: '*He ain't gonna like that she ain't dead.*'"

"Who ain't gonna like it?" asked Melinda.

"That is the sixty-four dollar question," said Lowell.

"What does that mean?" asked Johnny.

"It means that if we can find out who put a contract out on you we may be able to find out who killed Judge Winston."

"Christ, you really think there's a real contract on me?"

"Well, there may have been one in prison," said Lowell. "If it is extended to the outside we had better all watch our step. Johnny, you are not to go out alone under any circumstances. If you need something there will always be someone who will accompany you."

Johnny looked very nervous. "Well, what can I do? I mean, what the fuck is gonna happen to me?"

"You should be all right here," said Melinda.

Johnny looked around, unconvinced.

Lowell took out his cell phone and hit a few buttons.

"Roland," said the policeman.

"It's David Lowell."

"Yes, what can I do for you?"

"There was an event on Riker's yesterday."

"Yes, I'm familiar with it. Believe it or not we get phone calls, too."

"Well, I've bailed Johnny Colbert out and she's staying at my place."

The lieutenant must have smiled for the first time that day at the thought of that bad-tempered woman upsetting what he suspected was Lowell's delicate sense of equilibrium.

"How wonderful for you."

"Yes, I'm sure you think so. Anyway, people tried to kill her, and her defense would be rather moot if they succeeded."

"So what do you want me to do about it? Maybe she pissed someone off at Riker's with that smart mouth of hers."

"Maybe, but I can't babysit her all day long or I'll never get my work done."

"The police department isn't on your personal payroll and we're not obligated to protect anyone once they are out of the system."

"They did such a fine job of protecting her when she was in it, didn't they?"

The lieutenant sighed. "Well, you do have a point there. What do you want?"

"Just some extra drive-bys and a word to the cops in my neighborhood would be nice."

"Anything else, your highness?"

"That should be sufficient. I'll have Andy stay at the house whenever possible during the day, and he's licensed to carry a gun."

"Just make sure that's all he does with it. All right, I'll have a car stationed on your block periodically, but don't take advantage of the situation."

"Thank you, Lieutenant."

Lowell looked at Melinda, and then Johnny. "Please, no more trouble today."

Chapter Twelve

The next morning, Lowell was in the office when Sarah buzzed.

"Melinda on line one."

He picked up the phone. "How are things?"

"Not so good. Somebody wants this thing to go away, and quickly."

"You mean besides me?"

"You've been a gem, really. I can't tell you how much I appreciate what you're doing for Johnny. But they're putting our case on fast track."

"Well, that doesn't give us much time. What time can you be at the townhouse? I'd like to compare notes."

"I'm stuck at the courthouse until about six. This case has been taking up a lot of my time and I've got to catch up on my other clients. But I'll be home by seven."

"I'll send Andy to get you then."

The rest of Lowell's day was spent on chart analysis and dead-end pursuits. Everything was pointing to their client. There were very few leads.

Sarah came in to say she was going for the day. It was almost six. Lowell preferred to remain in the office for the duration of a case so he could stay on top of things and not get distracted. But Johnny was at the townhouse, and he felt he should get back before too long, even with Andy around and a cop car on the street.

Lowell took a cab uptown. As the cab drove down his street, he didn't see the cop car Roland had promised, nor did he see one at the other end of the street. He was disappointed but not surprised. The city was hurting financially and crime was up. Resources were stretched thin.

When he opened the front door, Julia was standing there, a frantic look on her face.

"Oh, Mr. Lowell, I'm so glad you are here. The woman sneaks out as soon as Mr. Andy leaves to pick up Melinda and I'm in the kitchen. I tried to keep an eye on her, but she asked me to get her some of my homemade lemonade. When I got up to get it, she must have left."

"How long ago?"

"Twenty minutes, no more. I'm sorry."

"Don't blame yourself. There was nothing you could do."

Lowell called Melinda. She was in the limo and arrived fifteen minutes later.

"Look," she said, "there's no reason to worry. Maybe she just went for a walk."

"I told her not to leave the house under any circumstances. Doesn't she understand that her life is in danger?"

"I don't know. I can't understand it."

Lowell didn't want to bring up his million-dollar bail at the moment.

Melinda shook her head. "How did she get out without setting off the alarm?"

"Remember you can open and close the door from the inside and slip out without triggering it if you do so quickly."

They were just about to call Lieutenant Roland when the phone rang. Lowell snatched it up.

"Hello… yes… well where are you…uh huh, we'll discuss that later. They did what… Okay, stay right where you are. No wait, go somewhere public… No, not a bar…Starbucks is fine. We'll pick you up there. Don't leave!"

He put the phone down and turned to an anxious Melinda and Julia.

"She went to her place to pick up some things. When she got there someone had trashed the place. That's all I know. We'll get the rest of the story from her."

Andy drove them downtown to East Eighth Street, where they found Johnny in the coffee store perched at a corner table trying to look inconspicuous, a beat-up green suitcase on the floor beside her. Melinda went to get her.

Johnny got into the limo and Lowell could see that her hands were shaking. "Do you have anything to drink?" she asked.

"What would you like? Coke, water?"

"Bourbon."

Lowell nodded and opened a small cabinet from which he removed a liter of Old Grand Dad and a tumbler. He poured two inches into it and handed it to Johnny, who proceeded to down it in one shot. She held out her hand and was rewarded with another double. This time she sipped it.

"Why did you leave?" asked Lowell.

"I had to get out. I was going crazy there. Suffocating. I just thought I could go to my place, get a few things and be back before anyone missed me. I got to my apartment and the door was open. The place had been trashed. I mean they ripped every fucking thing to shreds. My mattress, my chairs. The assholes. What did I do to deserve this?" She took another sip of the amber liquid. "I ran in and grabbed a few things and stuffed them in this suitcase. Then I was about to leave when I heard the front door of the building open and two men started running up the staircase. One saw me and said, *'There she is.'* So I ran down the back stairs and hid in an alley. They passed about a foot from me. If they had turned around I think I'd be dead."

She downed the second drink.

"What the fuck am I going to do? They trashed my whole fucking life."

Lowell noticed lottery tickets sticking out of Johnny's back jeans pocket. He didn't say anything. But he found it interesting that despite her recent brush with violence she still managed to stop at a bodega and buy those awful things.

They went back to the townhouse. Melinda agreed to stay over for a few nights to help keep an eye on Johnny. The two were in the den having drinks and snacks. Lowell had gone to bed.

"Where are you from?"

"I'm from a little shit town you've never heard of. Christ, you wouldn't even notice if you had passed through it. There's fewer than a thousand people living there and they got like twelve bars, and they're full all day and all night long."

"What did your father do?"

"You mean to me? Or for a living?"

"Was it bad?"

Johnny sipped her bourbon. "Sometimes. Sometimes it was real bad."

Her face tightened.

"He would hang out in the bars, especially when he wasn't working. Then he'd come home drunk and beat the crap out of me. He'd say things like *'I wanted a son. I'm going to make a man out of you if it kills you. Why don't you have a fucking dick?'* I guess some of it worked its way into me. I call myself Johnny." She half-smiled.

"So you came to New York."

"When I was eighteen he attacked me for the last time. I took a shovel and smashed him over the head a few times. It didn't kill him, but I wish it had. I knocked him out and cracked up his face pretty good though. I bet he's not so handsome anymore. I ran away that day and never looked back."

"What about your mother?"

"What about her? She never did anything to stop him, so what the fuck do I care about her?"

They sat in silence for a few minutes, sipping their cocktails.

"All night long I serve drinks to people who came to New York to become something—a Broadway star, a Wall Street big shot. I came to New York just to be. Just to be me."

She looked into Melinda's eyes.

"I swore to myself all those years ago that I would live my life, whatever it was, and make the most of it I could. And nobody would ever, *ever* put their hands on me again if I didn't want them to." She gulped the rest. "And now I got stuck in something I got nothing to do with, and they're still going to get me."

"No," said Melinda, "they're not."

Chapter Thirteen

Lowell had the morning news on one of the flat screens in the small downstairs office he maintained in the townhouse.

"Morning," said Johnny, as she stuck her head in.

"You're in a chipper mood."

"Well, I slept great on that amazing bed and hell, I feel terrific." She walked into the room before he could utter a protest. "Whatcha doing?"

"I'm looking over the astrology charts of the main characters in our little play." His desk was littered with several dozen charts and a large pile of perhaps fifty more waiting on the side.

Johnny picked one up.

"Hey, this is me. So how does this shi…stuff work?"

Lowell took the chart from her hand and returned it to the desk. "It's a little complicated."

"Well, can't you just give me the Cliff Note's version?"

Despite himself, the teacher within was forced to answer. "An oversimplification would be to say that astrology is a study of how everything in the universe is connected to everything else and how best to use that knowledge to improve your life. It gives us insight into the personality, and the physical and psychological makeup of the individual."

"Okay, so like, what are these numbers?" She picked the chart back up and pointing.

"Those represent the twelve Houses of the personal zodiac. Each House rules a number of things in our lives."

"But there are only twelve Houses, how could that stand for everything?"

"Many things are more closely related than you think."

"Give me an example. What does the 6th House mean?"

"Well, the 6th House rules health, your place of work, pets."

"Oh, and pets are supposed to be good for your health, right?"

"That's right."

"Also, if you like your job, that's probably better for you too, huh?"

Lowell nodded.

"Tell me more. What's the 1st House mean? And what's it got to do with, say the 2nd House or the 7th House?"

"The 1st House is you, your personality and the projection of your persona out to the world. The 2nd House is your money and your values. The opposite of the 1st House is the 7th House, which rules your partner, especially in business or marriage. What do you think the 8th House represents?"

Johnny looked down at the chart. "Your partner's money?"

Lowell was just a bit surprised. "That's right. Okay, if the 10th House rules your career, what would the 11th House rule?"

"I suppose the money you make from your career. But I know a lot of people who say their career is show business, but they never make any money from it. All they do is slop pigs just like me. So that might not be the money you earn every paycheck, right?"

"That's absolutely right."

"The money from the 11th House could maybe come from a painting you did twenty years before?"

Again he was stunned. He had tried to teach that very concept to students of the celestial arts for many months at a time only to meet with blank stares. Lowell smiled. "That's damn insightful. You're very bright."

"Oh I see, just because I'm a little punked out and I got a lion painted across my tits I must be a stupid bimbo, is that is?"

"Not at all…"

"Look, I know I got a mouth like a truck driver and I don't know how to act like a lady. I didn't get much of a chance. My old man smacked me around pretty good, and I had to leave school before I even got my high school diploma. But I finally did get it here in New York. I was almost thirty but I got it." The pride in her voice was unmistakable. "So just because I'm a little rough around the edges doesn't mean I'm stupid."

"But you misunderstood. I don't think you're stupid at all. The last person I taught who could grasp complete concepts in a single explanation was my daughter. Few get it so quickly as she did. You seem to have a bit of a gift for the celestial arts, and I was surprised, that's all."

"Okay, good. What else does the 11th House rule?"

"It rules many things, including: friends, long term goals, elected government officials."

"Tell me more. What does the 9th House rule, and why don't I have any planets in it?"

"Well, the 9th House rules higher education, religion, long journeys, foreigners, in-laws, and the higher mind."

"Sorry to interrupt, but you got any wine around here?"

"In that cabinet," he said, pointing behind her.

She opened the door and found about two dozen bottles. After selecting one she took a small corkscrew and expertly removed the cork. Then she grabbed a wineglass from the cabinet and poured herself a healthy glassful. "Very nice," she said, after sampling it. "Can I pour you some?"

"No, it's a little early for me."

She shrugged and drank some more.

"You drink a lot, don't you?"

"I'm a bartender. It goes with the territory."

She pulled up a chair and watched him work for a while. "You're, like really rich, huh?"

"I guess so."

"How'd you make it?"

He decided there was no harm sharing his story. "I began buying oil futures when they were trading $32 a barrel and sold them at $130. Then I bought them back again at $35 a barrel.

"How did you know to do that?"

He smiled. "Astrology. Pluto, the ruler of oil, had just entered Sagittarius, the sign of expansion and unrestricted growth, and I knew it would make the price of oil explode. Once Pluto left Sagittarius and entered Capricorn I knew the price of oil would temporarily drop precipitously."

"Wow. And you made all this money just from that?"

"Well, I also traded gold, currencies, soybeans, and more. Once I had a lot of money it was easier to make more. I just continued to enlarge my trades as they made a profit and my wealth increased."

"So, money comes to money, as they say."

"Sometimes."

"Wow, cool."

She sipped her wine. "Did you always have the ponytail?"

"I first grew it in my youth, and then cut it short for many years. I grew it back about ten years ago. Hair is an important means of expression for my generation."

"I know. You even have a musical about it."

He laughed.

They discussed astrology, philosophy, and rock 'n' roll. Johnny knew a lot of the music from the baby-boomer era and, to her surprise, David was a long-time fan of rock music.

Johnny was getting antsy. "Any chance of going back to my place so I can salvage whatever is left?"

"I think we can risk it."

He called Andy and together they took Johnny downtown to her apartment on East Third Street off First Avenue. Andy remained by the car while Lowell escorted her up the three flights to her apartment, or what was left of it.

It was, as she had said, a total mess. Nothing was left unscathed. The furniture was beaten and broken; the clothes were ripped into rags. There was very little left. David had assumed that whoever had done this was searching for something, but as he walked through the rubble and saw the extent of the damage, he thought perhaps this was not just a search mission, but one of intimidation.

One thing he did notice was the hundreds and hundreds of lottery tickets spewed all over the room. Some were in piles with rubber bands around them, others were mavericks tossed everywhere. He thought about discussing it, but there would be a better time to bring it up.

Johnny picked up the remains of her clothes, trying to recover what she could. They were about to leave when she spied a small notebook partially buried underneath the debris. She reached under some ripped up sheets and pulled the book out. It was still intact.

"Well," she said, flipping through the pages, "at least my poetry survived."

"Poetry?"

"Yeah. Why? I can't write poetry?"

Lowell shrugged. "Sure, I don't see why not."

Johnny picked up a few more things, tossed them all into a plastic bag, and they left.

"I have nothing now," she said, as they walked down the stairs.

Back in the limo she became uncharacteristically quiet. They rode back to the townhouse in silence.

When they were home, Lowell went down to the office and called Lieutenant Roland.

"Someone trashed Johnny Colbert's apartment and chased her out of the building. They destroyed everything."

"We got the warrant day before yesterday and searched it about four-thirty in the afternoon. We left it more or less as we found it. Nothing was damaged. A few things may have been out of place, but nothing like you're describing."

"Well, somebody tore it to shreds."

"I was going to call you anyway today. I thought you'd like to know that when we searched her place we did find a detonator just like the one used to kill the judge."

"Where did you find it?"

"In a shoebox on a shelf in her closet."

"Seems a bit fortuitous, doesn't it?" asked Lowell. "I assume you dusted it for fingerprints. Did you find any?"

"No."

"None at all?"

"No."

"Didn't you find that a little strange?"

"Not really. She was afraid we might find it and could tie it to her."

"But you did find it. In fact, you found it in her apartment. Why would she wipe off her fingerprints but leave it right where you could find it?"

"It was hidden," said the policeman.

"It was in a shoebox on a closet shelf where anyone could have found it. How long did it take your men to uncover this mastermind's hiding place?"

"Maybe she was planning to get rid of it and didn't expect us to catch up to her so fast."

"Maybe. And maybe someone else left it there just in case you looked. It just seems funny to me that someone would make and plant a bomb, avoid getting caught in the act, and then leave an extra detonator for anyone to find. Did you find any of the explosives in her apartment?"

"No, we didn't."

"And didn't that seem a bit odd to you that she would have a detonator and no explosives?"

"We assume she kept the plastique somewhere else."

"Why?"

"Maybe for safety purposes."

"Maybe."

"We sent the box to the lab for further analysis," said Roland. "If you like, I'll have someone email you a copy of the report."

"Thank you, I would appreciate that."

"Well, I just thought you'd like to know."

Lowell hung up just as Mort entered.

"That sounded interesting."

"That was Lieutenant Roland. They found a detonator in Johnny's apartment in a shoebox on a shelf in her closet."

"Wasn't that thoughtful of her to leave it there for them to find?"

Lowell nodded.

"Still, she is a little strange," said Mort, as he flapped his arms up and down.

"Yes, she is a little strange," said Lowell, as he watched his friend and tried hard not to laugh.

Chapter Fourteen

Rush hour was in full swing that evening as Melinda walked out of the courthouse. She was about to head uptown when Lowell walked up and took her arm.

"I thought I'd come down and escort you."

"Don't surprise me like that. Where's Andy?"

"Why don't we walk for a while," said Lowell. "I can call him anytime. He's in the neighborhood somewhere."

They strolled up Lafayette Street, an older, quieter part of the city, pretty much untouched by the recent massive wave of urban renewal and expansion that had taken over the consciousness of New York. Lowell liked it down here. There was something comforting about buildings that had been there for a hundred years or more.

"How is your investigation going?"

"Not so good. I spoke to Lieutenant Roland. They found a detonator when they searched her place."

"What?"

"It was left more or less out in the open so they could find it. It looks like it was planted."

"I'm worried. I really don't believe she did it, but I might not be able to prove it."

She took her dad's arm in hers and leaned against him as they walked uptown.

"Don't worry," he said. "We'll find a way out of this. It's just a matter of being prepared for what life can throw at you."

"I know. That's the same lesson you've been trying to teach me since I was a little girl."

"It's one of the few lessons that really count."

They walked a few blocks when they heard a voice behind them.

"Hey, buddy, got a light?"

Lowell and Melinda turned and faced a man with a short-nosed gun in his right hand.

"All right, just give me your wallet and nobody gets hurt."

"Sure pal," said Lowell, "just don't get crazy."

He took a wallet out of his coat pocket and started to hand it to the man.

"Dad, what are you doing?"

"Teaching you the same lesson again."

"Hey," said the gunman, "shut the fuck up and give me the wallet."

Lowell handed it to the man. He looked through it, saw a bunch of bills and credit cards, and smiled a satisfied grin. Then he ran down the street, clutching his prize like a street mongrel with a pilfered bone.

"Why did you give it to him?" asked Melinda, when the man had disappeared.

"It's all about being prepared. That was a wallet I bought on the street for five dollars. It has a few bucks, some phony mock-up paper credit cards and some false documents to give it the illusion of purpose."

"You had a decoy wallet with you? Why on earth would you?"

Lowell looked at her and smiled. "If you understood, I wouldn't have to keep teaching you the same lesson."

"You know, dad, you never cease to amaze me."

"And I hope I never do."

They continued walking up Lafayette Street, until they came to a small bistro housed on the bottom floor of an old building. Lowell stopped.

"This is where I first took your mother for coffee." He laughed. "I was so broke that when she ordered a cappuccino

I had to count my change to make sure I could afford to pay." He looked up at the grand old structure for a few minutes. "I wonder how long it'll take them to tear this down." Nostalgia washed over him like a warm summer rain. "Oh, well," he finally said, "let's move on."

About a block further north the same man came out of the side street.

"Hey," he shouted.

Lowell stopped and sighed. "What do you want now?"

"I want the real wallet. You think I'm stupid or blind?"

"Which question do you want answered first."

"Those credit cards are made of paper." The man pointed a gun at Lowell. "You think you're smarter than me?"

"I think my turtles are smarter than you."

"You need to be taught a lesson."

"That's just what I've been telling my daughter here."

The man approached.

"Dad?"

"I can handle this."

The man began waving the gun it in Lowell's face. "I'm going to teach you a lesson you'll never forget."

Lowell took his hand out of his pocket and extended his arm straight out. He was holding a piece of paper, which he let drop from his fingers. The paper drifted slowly toward the ground, distracting the gunman for only a moment, but that was all Lowell needed.

Suddenly the gun was no longer in the mugger's hand but in Lowell's. He dropped it into his pocket.

"You're going to teach me a lesson?"

The man dove at him, trying to punch Lowell in the mouth, but Lowell took one step to the side. As the man's fist went past his face, Lowell grabbed the man's arm. The man stumbled, but kept his footing. He went to grab Lowell by the throat with both hands. Lowell took the man's wrists and turned them inward as he stepped backward, forcing the man to his knees.

The guy looked up at Melinda, his face twisted in pain.

"Hey, lady, what is he? A cop?"

"No," said Melinda, "an astrologer."

They were all gathered at the townhouse for dinner. Lowell told Johnny about the package the police had found, and Johnny vehemently denied any knowledge of it.

"We believe you. We just need to find out who planted it." Melinda smiled at Johnny. "Tomorrow, I need to see your neighbor, Paula Osgood. The prosecution has her on its witness list."

"Are you deposing her in your office?" Lowell sipped his beer.

Melinda shook her head. "I thought it might be better to just do it casually. I told her I'd drop by her place. People tend to be more honest and open when they feel at ease."

"I don't understand what she has to do with this," said Johnny.

"I have to talk to everyone on the prosecution's list, and they've added Mrs. Osgood."

"She's a busybody nosy pain in the butt that's always complaining about everything and trying to start trouble with me. What does she have to do with this?"

"That's what I have to find out. They're going to use every nasty means to try and destroy your character. My job is to be prepared when we enter the courtroom."

"Until you've worked in a bar, you don't know what nasty is."

Chapter Fifteen

Melinda took a sip of her deli coffee, announced herself over the intercom, and walked up the three flights. A short, stocky woman with bleached hair answered the door.

"Mrs. Osgood, how nice of you to receive me."

The woman snorted. "Like I had a choice."

She was wearing jeans at least one size too small and a tank top that exposed her generous midsection.

They sat in the living room on the couch. Melinda turned on a small tape recorder and then took out her pad and began reading her prepared questions.

"You know the defendant, Joanna Colbert?"

"I certainly do. She lives across the hall from me."

"Can you tell me what kind of neighbor she is?"

"It's just like I told that prosecutor guy. She's a loud-mouthed drunk, always coming home at two or three in the morning waking me up. She has a nasty attitude and brings home strange men. I've had to call the police several times complaining about noise and parties. I ain't a saint, but there's such a thing as being good neighbors."

"Mrs. Osgood, my client works nights. You are aware of that?"

"Sure, like all whores."

"Actually she works as a bartender, often sixty hours a week or more, and that's why she comes home late at night."

The woman shrugged.

"Would you say that she has a temper?"

"Like a mad dog."

"Has Ms. Colbert ever been aggressive with you?"

"Lord, yes. Last year I was trying to take my garbage out and she almost threw me down the stairs. That's when I called the cops. I had bruises for weeks."

"Isn't it true that on the occasion in question it was you who actually began the altercation with my client? That you had started the day by banging on her door at eight in the morning knowing that she worked until almost four?"

"She woke me up in the middle of the night. I felt it was only fair."

"And when my client asked you to stop, you threatened her, isn't that also true?"

"I did not," said the woman, indignantly.

"Didn't you tell her that, quote, *'Your nephew had "friends" who would take care of her'?"*

"I was afraid of her. She's one tough bitch. Sure I told her about my nephew. She's an animal."

"And wasn't it you that tried to throw her down the stairs?"

"I was the one that called the police, not her."

"But when the police came and heard both sides of the story they refused to press charges."

"They're all a bunch of pussies. Said it was between us and we would have to work it out."

"In fact, you've called the police a total of fourteen times regarding my client. And in each one of those cases they left without issuing a single warrant or filing any papers beyond your initial complaint. Why is that?"

"Because she's skinny and has tits," said the woman. "And that's all men can see."

Melinda remained silent.

"She's also a hard-ass nasty woman with a lousy temper and no regard for anyone else," continued the woman, her voice climbing to a crescendo.

"Seems to me that you have quite a temper yourself," said Melinda.

"You try living across the hall from her, you'll have one, too."

"I think you've always had this temper."

The woman leaned forward in the chair. "I don't like being pushed around." She glared at Melinda.

"I can see that. Are you aware that someone broke into my client's apartment and trashed it, tearing up virtually everything she owned?"

"Really, now isn't that just terrible."

"You wouldn't know anything about that?"

"Why ask me?"

"It just seems strange that you are so sensitive to noise and yet didn't hear anything while her apartment was being trashed."

"I must have been out when it happened."

"Just one more question. You'd be very happy if Johnny Colbert moved out, wouldn't you?"

"I'd be lying if I said no."

"And if she is convicted, she will no longer be your neighbor, isn't that right?"

"God, I pray that's so. I hope they throw her in jail for the rest of her life."

Chapter Sixteen

Lowell was on the office phone putting in his morning trades. "Buy ten November gold at the market and get me a price on 1400 calls."

"You bullish on the metals again?"

"Somewhat. Keep an eye on the spreads. Once they start moving you can be sure this is going up."

"Okay," said Roger Bowman, "I'll watch it. How about coming down for lunch soon?"

"Maybe when this trial is over. I've got my hands full right now."

"I understand."

"How are things down there?"

"Well, I'm one of the lucky ones," said Roger. "I've still got a job."

"Bad, huh."

"Blood running in the streets. It's the worst thing since '29 and you, you son of a bitch, predicted the whole damn mess."

"Not me; astrology."

"Too bad nobody would listen, huh?"

"I'm not sure it would have made any difference. Listen Roger, I've got a dilemma you might be able to help me with. You're a bit of a gambler, aren't you?"

"I work on Wall Street, what do you think?"

"I mean other types of gambling, you know, like games."

"I've been known to visit a casino on occasion. Why? Are you looking for a comp? I know some people at Foxwoods."

Lowell laughed. "Hardly. I have a client with a bit of a gambling problem and I'm trying to get a handle on it, that's all."

"What's the client's thing?"

"State lotteries, daily numbers, scratch-off tickets, and all that kind of crap."

"Oh boy," said Roger. "I think there's someone you should talk to. Her name is Sally Rogers. We dated briefly about five years ago. I think she can answer most of your questions. She used to work for the state lottery commission."

"Who does she work for now?"

"Gamblers Anonymous."

"Why did you break up?"

"Her friends started to call me Roger Rogers."

"Oh, hello," she said, extending her hand. "Roger told me you were coming. Won't you sit down?" She was an attractive woman with long brown hair and big eyes painted a subtle purple color. She was dressed in jeans and a peasant blouse, her feet were bare. Lowell smiled only a little, as his ex-wife dressed like this when they first met.

"It was very nice of you to see me on such short notice."

"Don't be silly. Anything I can do to help."

The apartment was a small one bedroom in a pre-war walk-up building on 28th Street off 12th Avenue. The floors slanted about a few degrees. The kitchen, what there was of it, ranged against one wall in the living room.

Lowell sat in the only armchair in the room. Sally sat on the couch.

"Roger tells me you're an astrologer detective."

Lowell nodded.

"Well, that's an interesting profession. Are there many like you?"

"Not that I know of."

"How can I help you?"

Lowell explained his situation, without mentioning his client's name.

"The state lotteries in this country," she began, "are one of the unmentioned plagues that afflict our nation. Did you know that Thomas Jefferson refused to institute lotteries, calling them 'a tax on the poor'? How right he was."

"So tell me a little about how this works."

"Well, the purpose is to raise money for education, although whose bright idea it was to connect gambling with teaching I don't know. The plan, obviously, is to make as much money as they can. To that end the lottery hires people with all sorts of specialties, including advertisers, art designers, statistics experts, behavioral specialists, psychologists, and such."

"Psychologists?"

"Sure. That's what my master's degree is in. They had one woman they got from N.Y.U. who specialized in addiction as a disease. After teaching for sixteen years and becoming an expert on what makes people addicts, she was offered five times her salary to bring that expertise to the lottery, where she advises them on the most addictive colors, numbers, and various games."

Lowell shook his head.

Sally continued. "But they don't really even have to bother. People will buy them anyway. These tickets are like a candy to anyone who is bipolar, has attention deficit disorder, is obsessive compulsive, angry, depressed, has a bad marriage or an overdue electric bill. The poor especially run for these things. They see it as the only way out of a terrible situation. But of course for almost all of them it just makes matters that much worse."

She let out a deep breath, as though she had held that one in for a long time.

"They'll run out in ten-degree weather with the flu. In the middle of a snowstorm to play their lucky numbers. God forbid it comes in the one day they don't play it. They can't pass a store without buying at least one ticket. They have to have every scratch-off that has their favorite number. It's as horrible a sickness as I've ever seen. Do you know what the odds are of winning anything worth mentioning?"

"I do."

"Disgraceful isn't it?"

"Yes," said Lowell, "But I can understand the allure of a million dollar payday, no matter how small the chance."

"And then if by some miracle they do win something big, more often than not it ruins their lives. Now you know why I live in a walk-up and work for Gamblers Anonymous. I didn't sleep the whole four years I worked for them."

"I understand."

"Do you know how much money the state takes in each year? Almost four billion dollars. And that's only the scratch-off tickets. Have you seen the people line up with their lotto and a list of numbers as two pages long?"

"I have, actually."

"And they say it's all in the name of education." Sally shook her head. "It would be cheaper to charge the poor people money to send their kids to a good school than to steal it from them this way."

"There's nothing worse than wishing for something you'll never be able to get."

"They have a scratch-off that costs thirty dollars. Can you believe it? You want to guess what the payoff is?"

Lowell shook his head.

"A million dollars a year for life. A million goddamn dollars a year, for as long as you live. It's astounding. And all the poor bastards run to get them."

She took a Marlboro from a hard pack and lit it, trying to blow the smoke away from Lowell.

"Sorry, it's a nasty habit, I know. When I started it was still cool. Now I'm like a pariah."

She took a deep puff and then put it out. "Do you know what front-loading is?"

Lowell waited.

"When they put out a new scratch-off game, they put a lot of winners in the front packs, especially fifty and a hundred dollar winners. That way a lot of gamblers win on it and the word gets out that this is a hot game. Of course, by the time you get to the store it's already too late. The front runners have bought them all and yours are losers."

She walked over to the window, opened it and tried to push the smoke outside.

"How badly off is your client?"

"She has an addictive personality."

"Alcohol or drugs?"

"Alcohol."

"It's often one or the other. It breaks down the person's resistance to their gambling temptation. Eventually you have to deal with both. But one thing at a time. The addictions are all really the same, anyway. If we can get them into the program, we can address the other issues in time. Go on."

"She's deeply in debt to credit cards and seems unable to extricate herself from the situation."

Sally shook her head with great exaggeration. "Credit cards. Don't let me get started on those horrible things. Tell me something. Do you have credit cards?"

"Of course."

"Yes, of course you do. You can't live in America without them. They made sure of that. And do you pay them off in total every month?"

"Absolutely," said Lowell, "without fail."

"You know, in the banking business they have a name for people like you who take care of your debts each month. You know what they call you?"

"What?"

"Deadbeats. But you're in the minority. I have to do a lot of work helping my people with their credit cards and the debts they have accumulated."

"What's that like?"

"You wouldn't believe me if I told you. The whole purpose of credit cards is to keep the individual in debt his entire life. That's why they used to raise your credit limit even if you were already in debt. They don't want *you*, someone who pays them off every month, as a client. You won't make them any money. That's why you're called a deadbeat. They want overstretched workers, soccer moms in a rush, and families with expensive health issues, anything that will keep them in debt. And of course, that's all changed temporarily, now that the bottom fell out. It all collapsed into itself, as was bound to happen."

Lowell nodded, remembering his own past, before his reversal in fortune, when he, too, was in debt.

"And many of them, regular people you would never think of as degenerates, have a gambling problem. They take cash advances off the credit cards and spend it on lotto, scratch-offs, horse racing, casinos, and the like. We're swamped with opportunities to win huge amounts of money. Unfortunately most wind up losing much more than they can afford. They destroy their lives with this garbage."

"What can be done?"

"Thankfully there are counseling programs designed to help. That's what we try to do at Gamblers Anonymous. It's an addiction like any other and should be treated as such. It's up to the individual to reach out and take the aid, but it's there in most big cities."

"We always were a nation of risk-takers. I guess they've just tapped into that need and mined it for all it's worth."

She shook her head in disgust and disbelief. "Did you know that there is now a Monopoly set that has no cash? It's all done by credit card. You transfer funds from one player to another. As Steven Stills said: *teach your children well.* What's happened to America? What's the hell has happened? You're an astrologer." It wasn't a question. "What do you think is going to happen to our country? Will it get better? My mother is eighty-five and told me the other day that she never thought she'd have to live through another depression. She's scared, and so am I. Will we be able to stabilize things and regain some sense of fair play and balance, or just watch as the middle class and the American dream continue to deteriorate?"

Lowell had been taking all this in. "I believe that America is fundamentally strong and will survive. Unquestionably the world has reached a crossroads where we must make some very difficult decisions, and I do have serious doubts that we will make the right ones. But I have hope."

He handed her a card.

"I'm giving a lecture on the political and financial future of America on the fifteenth of this month at the Ivy League Club. I think you'll find it interesting. If you email my secretary she'll put you on my mailing list."

"I have a friend who is very into this stuff. Maybe I will come and bring her."

Lowell stood up. "I want to thank you. You've been most helpful and informative."

Sally stood as well. "If there's anything else I can do for you please let me know. One of the real limitations with addictive problems is that people are often ashamed of them and try to solve them alone. It would be better to go to someone who has experience with such things."

Chapter Seventeen

Lowell, Melinda, and Johnny met in the office for a light lunch and to compare notes.

Sarah knocked and entered.

"Sarah, come in, come in." Lowell picked up her astrology chart and said: "How is your lower back feeling?"

"It's much better now. Hey, I never mentioned my back. Don't do that, it freaks me out."

Lowell laughed. "Sorry, I'm just working on an experiment and I was using your chart. You want to be part of it?"

"Does it involve getting shot at?"

"No."

"Then count me in."

"Good."

He took two hundred-dollar bills from his wallet and handed them to her.

"Between exactly 2:14 and 2:22 I want you to buy some tickets like you did the other day. Venus is conjunct your part of fortune today and the Moon will be applying to a conjunction of that point exactly at that time. I want to see how that plays out. Now, what time do you have?'

Sarah looked at her phone. "1:52."

"Perfect. Now remember, only buy them from 2:14 until 2:22, and then stop."

Sarah left on her mission and David went back to his computer.

"What's he doing?" asked Johnny.

"He's trying to beat the system," said Melinda.

"He can do that? I mean is that possible?"

"I don't know." She started to laugh. "But if anyone can, it's him."

"With astrology?"

Melinda laughed loudly.

Lowell looked up. "What's so funny?"

"You are," said his daughter. "It must be very exciting in that head of yours for you to follow all these threads."

"I have to know everything about a subject before I can make an educated decision."

"Yes, I know."

Johnny was playing with the turtles. Melinda walked over to the tank and stuck her finger out for Buster and Keaton to sniff.

"They're big," said Johnny.

"Each time I come here they seem a little larger."

"Yes," said Lowell. "It's about time to go shopping for a new turtle condo."

"Ooh, can I come along?" said Johnny. "I love pet stores."

"What? We'll see," said Lowell, brusquely.

"Maybe we could, um, go to the zoo in Central Park too? I love animals."

"Johnny," Lowell reprimanded her, "you're on trial for your life. I would think you would have more important things on your mind that going to the zoo."

She shrugged. "Whatever." Then she smiled at Lowell.

Melinda looked sideways at Johnny, then at her father. Could it be? Did Johnny have a thing for him? She smiled at the notion. Just have to watch and wait.

Sarah returned a few minutes later with a handful of colorful scratch-off tickets. She placed them in the middle of the desk and everyone came over.

"You did exactly as I told you?"

"I can tell time, boss."

"Okay, let's all get to it."

It was Melinda who first shrieked and held up a $500 winner. They all looked at it with astonishment. There was another $500 winner, a $100 winner, two fifties, four twenties and an assortment of ones and fives that added up to $1,311.

"Can you do that every time?" asked Johnny, her eyes wide open in excitement and just a bit of drool escaping from the side of her mouth.

"I don't have enough data," replied the astrologer. "I suppose with enough research we could map out the best times to gamble. Of course with the odds in this *dreadful* game being so horrendous this experiment would probably work better in a casino or racetrack. But remember, it will only work at all if you play only when it is time and quit the second that time passes."

"Can we do it again?" asked Sarah.

"Well, I'll look over everyone's charts and see when the next window of opportunity is coming. Now if you all don't mind, we have a defense to prepare."

"My God," said Melinda, as if snapping out of a trance. "Look at the time. I've got to get down to my office."

"What about me?" asked Johnny.

Lowell and Melinda exchanged a glance.

"I want you to go back to the townhouse and stay there," said Lowell, in a stern voice.

"Don't worry, I wouldn't go out alone now for anything."

Lowell buzzed Andy in the car. "I'm sending Johnny down to you. Get her to the townhouse and then come right back here."

"But boss, I thought you wanted me to stay with her?"

"She'll be all right for a few hours with Julia. And I need you."

After Melinda and Johnny left he picked up the intercom and pushed number two.

Mort entered a few minutes later. "What's up?"

"Have you found anything yet?"

"Nothing you couldn't have found through Google yourself."

"I think it's time to return to her apartment. I want you to get into her computer and let's see what's there."

"Did you happen to notice what kind of computer she had?"

He pulled his small notebook from his jacket pocket. "It was a Dell. The model was XPS 8100."

"Good."

Chapter Eighteen

When Andy returned he drove Lowell and Mort to the judge's residence. He parked up the street to wait while the two entered the building.

As they approached the concierge's desk, Lowell noted how quickly the crew had completed the lobby. The only trace of the chaos that had confronted him on his last visit was a sole workman still toiling next to the stairwell. There was a two-foot hole in the wall from which he had extracted a large wire cable that was actually many wires bundled together.

The same concierge was on duty.

"May I help you, gentlemen?"

"David Lowell." He presented his business card. "We met the other day. I'm working on Judge Winston's murder investigation."

The man took his card and placed it down without looking at it. "Yes, Mr. Lowell, I remember you."

"My associate and I require access to the apartment once again."

"I'm sorry," said the man, with little, if any, sympathy in his voice, "but I have been informed that you are no longer to be allowed in Ms. Winston's apartment."

Lowell's temper flared. "What do you mean, *you've been informed*? By whom have you been so instructed? The court of New York has granted me permission to inspect that apartment."

"Mr. Lowell, I'm sorry, but there isn't anything I can do to help you. I must ask you to please leave the premises at once or I shall be forced to call the police."

Lowell was just about to tell him to do so when Mort tugged at his sleeve. David looked over at him. He was shaking his head so slightly it would have been missed by someone who didn't know him. Lowell raised his eyebrows and Mort smiled a Mona Lisa grin.

"All right, but we'll be back with a court order."

"Have a nice day," said the concierge, turning his back on them.

"So?" asked David, once they were outside the building.

"Do you want to wait until the courts intervene?"

Lowell shook his head. "I want to get into that computer now. Time is not on our side, and there's always a chance that whoever put through the order to prevent our entrance has the clout to block us permanently."

Mort smiled. "Did you notice the man working on the electrical system?"

"Of course I did. I'm not blind."

"I took a look at the schematics of this building online before we left the office. Unless I'm mistaken, the cable he was repairing controls the security system, including the alarms and cameras. That includes the elevators and stairwells."

"Surely you're not suggesting that we break into the building and sneak up the staircase like a pair of common thieves, are you?"

"Of course not," replied Mort. "I'm horrified that you think I would suggest breaking the law."

They walked out of the condo and turned right, then circled around to the side of the building. There was a door in the middle of the block.

Lowell looked at Mort. "Well?"

It took Mort less than a minute to pick the lock They slipped through and scurried into the stairwell.

They climbed the stairs to the victim's apartment, the first three flights quickly; the last three, not so quickly. By the time they reached the sixth floor Lowell had resolved to return to the gym.

The apartment was close to the doorway they exited. The lock to the apartment door was trickier. It was a fool-proof, double bolt drop lock, made of titanium, with a life-time guarantee against burglary. It took Mort almost two minutes to pick it.

"How do you do that?"

"I don't know. It's like I'm inside the lock and I just know how to twist the pick just right."

Once inside they hurried to the computer and Lowell handed Mort a pair of latex gloves.

"What about you?"

"I was already allowed up here, so finding my fingerprints will be expected.

Mort turned on the computer.

"What's your first impression of this place?" Lowell looked around and gestured for Mort to do the same.

The psychic turned around and looked at the sterile room for a few moments. "Nobody lived here."

"That's what I thought, too."

Mort was able to break the password quickly, but there were firewalls protecting some files that were more difficult.

"Obviously these are the ones we want," said Lowell, looking over Mort's shoulder. "Can you get into them?"

"You didn't hire me for my good looks and witty repartee, but a few files are encrypted with a self-destruct program, and they would take some time to bypass."

"Is there anything you can do quickly?"

Mort took out a screwdriver from a small canvas bag. "Only one thing I can think of right off the top of my head." He shut the machine off, bent down, and pulled the computer out from under the desk. He unscrewed the casing and took the front off. Then reached into his bag and pulled out a black metal rectangle.

"What's that?" asked Lowell.

"It's a blank, formatted hard drive, the same that comes standard with this model. With luck, this way it will look like someone erased the files from the original one. With a little more luck nobody will know that it's missing."

He gently pulled out a sliding drawer, removed the rectangle's twin, put the decoy in its place, screwed it in, and put the casing back on. Then he pushed the computer back to where it had been. He put the treasure in his bag and they headed for the door.

◇◇◇

The concierge walked over to the workman. "How much longer will you be? Some of the residents have complained."

The workman was sitting on the floor; a ten-foot stretch of coaxial cable extended out from a hole in the wall like the umbilical cord of some strange electronic creature. He looked up at the concierge. "Fuck 'em." He said it with the strength of his union to back him up. "It'll take as long as it takes."

"You have until exactly five o'clock. Then I will call your supervisor."

"Don't get your ass in an uproar. I'll be done."

The concierge looked at his watch. "It's 4:40. I expect this appendage out of sight and that gaping hole sealed up in twenty minutes. You can come back tomorrow and finish whatever else needs to be done."

"Yeah, yeah, don't worry. I just got to run a test to see if the cameras are working."

He turned on the system, then went behind the concierge's desk and turned on the console. Eighteen screens lit up. There were ninety separate cameras throughout the building; each screen servicing two in a constant rotation. They would have to be all tested individually, but not tonight.

"All right, all I got to do is put it back into the wall and do a run-through and make sure the system's working. I'll send someone to repair the hole in the morning. Why don't you just put a couch or something in front of it for now? Should have a full view of everything in about ten minutes."

"You're not leaving until I get a chance to test this also."

"Yeah, whatever you say, buddy. Anything after five is time and a half. I'll stay here all night if you want. Let's test one part of the system to make sure it's working."

"Which one?"

"It doesn't matter," replied the workman, "you decide."

"The stairwells."

◇◇◇

Lowell closed the apartment door quietly and wiped off Mort's fingerprints. It was getting late in the afternoon and people would begin returning from work or school at any time. He didn't want to be seen by anyone who could identify them later. Breaking and entering, theft and God knows what other felonies they had committed might be just a bit difficult to explain. Besides, there was no way of knowing who had issued the restriction on his movement, and until he did know he had to be extra careful. An attempt had been made on his client's life. These people were playing for keeps. It wouldn't be wise to let them get him into a jail cell.

"Should we risk the elevators?"

Lowell shook his head. "The stairs. It's safer, and going down is much easier than coming up."

A door was opening down the hall. The two scurried into the stairwell just as a neighbor headed for the elevator.

They moved quickly down the steps.

◇◇◇

"Almost ready over here," said the workman. "Wait one second until I reconnect this last plug." He pushed the heavy cable into its appropriate input and fed the massive cord back into the wall where it lived. "All right, I'm ready. Just turn on the system and push the red reboot button on top. You should get a picture in about thirty seconds. Then punch up each stairwell camera one at a time and use the sweep."

Lowell and Mort were on the third floor. Mort looked up at the camera in the corner of the ceiling and noticed a flickering green light. "Uh oh, it looks like they're turning the system back on."

They started running downstairs two steps at a time.

"You getting anything yet?"

"It's all a little foggy."

"Just a second," said the workman. He reached into the wall and jiggled the cable a bit. "How's that?"

"Now it's coming into focus." The concierge looked down at the screens in front of him and started fiddling with the cameras.

Lowell and Mort had reached the street level. Lowell slowly opened the door and peered out. A security guard making his rounds was resting right outside, his back to the door. Lowell pulled his head back in and shut the door silently. He put his finger to his lips. Mort nodded.

"Just let me run through the stairwell cameras quickly and you can go."

He turned the knobs and had a full view of the Seventeenth floor staircase. The cameras were each on a movable apparatus that was controlled from here. He flipped each button and watched as the panoramic view was completed. First the Seventeenth floor, then the Sixteenth…

Mort looked up and saw that the light on the camera was no longer flickering and was now a solid green. He pointed. Lowell nodded and shrugged. They both moved out of the camera's range. It sat stationary atop its perch, but they knew that soon it would be moving back and forth, capturing the whole area.

Lowell opened the door again, very slowly. The man was still standing there. Lowell gently closed the door.

"Should we try for the basement?" whispered Mort.

"I have an idea." He took out his cell phone and was pleasantly surprised to see that he had a signal.

"I'm almost done," said the concierge. "Only three more floors to check out and you can leave."

The third-floor cameras were working fine. The second floor as well. He turned the knob on the ground floor stairwell cameras. There was someone in the stairwell. There appeared to be two men. He focused the camera and was about to zoom in on the faces.

A loud crash outside the building grabbed his attention. Horns were blasting and someone was shouting obscenities.

"Damn," he said, as he ran out from behind his desk and hurried to the front door. "What now?"

When he heard the crash the security guard also immediately headed for the front of the building.

The scene outside was chaos. A limousine driver had apparently smashed his car into a double-parked car.

The concierge ran up to the driver. "Hey, you've got to get this thing out of here."

"This guy backed up into me," said Andy. "Look at that damage. I'm not paying for that."

The other driver was shouting back. "I did no such thing. He ran right into the back of my car."

"I don't see any damage to your car at all," said Andy.

"Look, I don't care," said the concierge, "you've just got to clear the front of this building or I'll call the cops."

Andy pointed at the other driver. "You're just lucky I'm in a hurry."

"I didn't do anything," the other man protested.

Andy got in the limo and drove away. He picked up his two little bandits around the corner.

Chapter Nineteen

They returned to the midtown office. Work was Lowell's stabilizer, and whether in his office, the limo, or at home, he needed to be busy and focused. A multitasker, he could concentrate on several issues at the same time, alternating between them in an unbroken stream of consciousness. It was not good for his mind to remain idle for any length of time.

Lowell took the hard drive out of Mort's bag and put it on the desk.

"Let's see what it's all about."

Mort opened the casing to one of Lowell's computers and exchanged the drives. Then he booted the machine and started working on the firewalls.

"This is one of the most complex security systems I've encountered in a long time."

After a bit of typing, tinkering, and muttering to himself, he turned to David. "Eureka."

Lowell gave him a sideways glance.

"I always wanted to say that."

"What have you got for me?"

"Well, it looks like Judge Winston was not going to be presiding over debtor's court for much longer."

"What makes you say so?"

"I could only get into one file so far," said Mort, his head bobbing with excitement as he talked. "Whoever programmed these defenses was quite creative. They've set it up as a maze, with many false turns. It's going to take me some time to break through all of them. But I did get to this."

He turned on the printer and hit the print button. A moment later he took a piece of paper from the tray and handed it to Lowell. "If I'm not mistaken, this is a list of political donors."

Lowell took the sheet of paper and perused it. It was a list of twenty names with a dollar amount next to each, the smallest being one million dollars. "Well, this *is* rather impressive. This is an A-1 group of some of the top Republican money people in the country. I count no fewer than five billionaires, and all willing to back an unknown entity. They must have had a lot of faith in this woman. I would say she was being groomed for a political career in the Republican Party. And I think they had very big plans for her."

"How big?"

"I don't know. Maybe as big as they get."

"Do you think this had something to do with her murder?"

"I wouldn't be surprised. The ruler of her 11th House was being afflicted at the time of her death, and that has much to do with political issues. Still, the indicators are that no matter what other motivations may have been present, this murder seems to have been more about money than anything. I hate to say it, but…"

"We're going to have to do some more actual work?"

"And I think I know where to start."

Rosen ushered them into his office.

"Mr. Lowell, nice to see you again so soon."

"This is my colleague, Mort Simpson."

Rosen nodded politely. They sat.

"There are just a few more questions," said Lowell, taking out the list of donors. "First of all, could you explain this to me? It came into my possession only yesterday and I thought perhaps you could shed some light on its meaning."

He pushed the paper across the desk.

Rosen glanced down at it with instant recognition, and shock.

"Of course," he quickly regained his composure. "This is a list of pledged contributors to the Judge's future political career. How did you get this? I must congratulate you. It's supposed to be a well-kept secret. Apparently you are a man of some resources."

"How we got it isn't important. Is there some reason you didn't mention this to me the first time we met? Didn't you think it warranted discussion in a murder trial?"

"For one thing," said Rosen, pushing the paper back toward Lowell with a bit more force than was necessary, "within certain political circles this is all common knowledge. There was nothing underhanded or manipulative. But it isn't fodder for the public. At least not yet. These are private matters that are of no concern to you. Second, there is no reason to seek an alternative motive. The police have the murderer, and despite your best efforts to redirect attention where it doesn't belong, they are going to convict her."

"So this prominent group of extremely wealthy corporate giants, bankers, and political heavyweights had decided to put their rather robust support behind an unknown?"

"In case you haven't noticed, that is the way things are going these days. Nobody trusts Washington, so everyone is looking for outsiders they can push into office. It makes perfect sense to me."

"Try and sneak the candidates in before anyone knows anything about them, is that it?"

"Mr. Lowell, this country is in a war for its survival. It is a war of ideology in a time when moral deterioration has reached a place of crisis. If the people do not elect the proper rulers to represent their best interests in Washington, I'm afraid our vast society will continue to crumble until we are only a shell of our former greatness. If it requires sidestepping the very system that has been failing, why not?"

"Yes, I think I'm beginning to understand. But why choose Farrah Winston?"

"She was exactly what was needed at this point in history. A young, beautiful woman raised in a strict conservative household with a Republican lineage that runs back generations. One of the next presidents of the United States will most likely be a woman. After a term in the Senate or the House, Farrah would have been just right."

"She was going to run for Senate?"

Rosen nodded. "Eventually. As you can see from that list, a lot of people believed in her."

"From New York?"

"Are you crazy? She was all set to move back to Utah. She kept a residence there and even flew back to vote each fall. But now that dream is over."

That explains why there was so little of a personal nature in her new apartment, thought Lowell. *She wasn't planning on being there very long.*

"And when she embarked upon her new career, were you were going to be on her team?"

"I can safely say that she felt I was indispensable. I would have been more than just on her team. I would have helped run it. She needed someone whose values she could rely on. We have very little time left to fix what is broken. The future is now."

"The future is now?" repeated Lowell. "That sounds vaguely familiar. Is that your philosophy?"

"That has always been my perspective. There just aren't a lot of people who truly understand that concept."

"And you do?"

"Yes, I understand it. I will do whatever it takes to prevent the moral destruction of America."

"Whatever it takes," repeated Lowell.

"Was there anything else?"

Lowell and Mort stood.

"No," said Lowell, "I think that's it. Thank you for your time."

"Well, what did you think?" asked Lowell when they were settled in the limo.

"I think he believed every word he said," replied Mort. "And I think he's just a wee bit psychotic."

"I agree."

"He also has a problem with his right knee."

Lowell laughed. "You know, he said one word that told me all I needed to know."

"What word was that?"

"When he was talking about the power struggle in America, he said how important it is for the people to elect the proper *rulers*, not leaders."

"Interesting choice of words."

"But not accidental. I also think he believes everything he said. He believes there is a cultural war going on in this country, and sees conspiracy everywhere. He is an extremist who thinks that only his philosophy is the right one. That may qualify him as a zealot. Quite a dangerous perspective."

"So, what do you think?"

Lowell was gazing out the window as the city flew by.

"This goes much deeper than I thought. According to what Rosen just told us, we may be looking at the assassination of a future political candidate."

"Is that possibility in her chart?"

"As with us all, only the potential. But yes, she had the chance to have an amazing career no matter what she chose to do."

"So, maybe she wasn't killed over a few credit card debts."

"No, said Lowell, "maybe not."

Chapter Twenty

That night, Melinda and David were eating at Louie's on East Thirty-third Street. Louie was an old hippie who had inherited the building that now housed his all-organic restaurant. The menu had a large vegetarian section that suited David. And the organic wines and beers were top notch.

"What's next?" asked Melinda.

"Well, there are a few leads, but so far not much to go on. I'll follow up on Larry Rosen. I'm sure he had something to do with all of this, but just how much, or if he was directly involved in the murder, I don't know."

Melinda put her fork down and sighed. "Frankly, if we can't establish reasonable doubt, I don't know what we can do for Johnny."

Lowell saw the anguish in his daughter's eyes. He had to admit how dark things looked for their client.

"So where do we stand?

"We know that someone murdered Judge Farrah Winston for reasons unknown. We assume that person or persons unknown waited until they had a reasonable fall guy, in this case, our client, who fit the profile. We know that an attempt on Johnny Colbert's life was carefully orchestrated on Riker's Island by person or persons unknown."

"So we don't know much, do we?"

"We also know that it was fate that you were handed this case. Otherwise Johnny Colbert would most certainly be facing life imprisonment."

"Well, if she was set up, can't we work backwards and see who had the opportunity and motive."

"That's what I'm trying to do," said Lowell. "But the more I look into Farrah Winston's past the less likely it seems that someone had it in for her. She was affable, well liked, and professional in her work. There is no hint of corruption or competition. Her personal life seems to have been quite tame."

"It doesn't look that good for Johnny, does it?"

"Not very. But don't worry. I've still got a few tricks up my sleeve." He chose not to mention now that he had committed B&E to get the judge's hard drive. He knew that what they might find couldn't be used in court, but it could help lead to other, usable evidence.

"I remember when you could solve things with just that old ratty ephemeris you used to carry around. It had so much tape holding the binding together I'm surprised you could still turn the pages."

"There's nothing ratty about it. Even with computers astrologers still often need to know the placement of the planets for weeks, even years at a time. Using a physical ephemeris lets me flip back and forth in time. I still use it almost every day."

"The same one?"

"Sure. I bought that book in Cambridge in 1975. I wouldn't part with it for the world. Besides telling me where all the planets are each day of the twentieth century, it holds the karma of so many of my early clients. Of course I have a new one for the twenty-first century. But times have changed. Do you think I could run my business without computers? I need both. I look at several hundred charts a week, sometimes fifty in a day. It used to take me an hour just to draw each one. I couldn't keep up if the computer didn't do the math for me."

Melinda patted her father's hand. "You're still my hero, Dad."

◇◇◇

They finished their meal and left the restaurant. It was Andy's day off so they had driven Lowell's Prius downtown. The sky looked dark and threatening, so they hurried to the spot on the street they had scored. Lowell prided himself on not paying for a parking garage, and he could parallel park like a pro.

The chilly rain pelted the car. He pressed the unlock button on his ring and the car lights flashed.

"Oh, hell, I got a ticket." He reached around to the windshield at what he thought was the orange envelope that New Yorkers had come to hate.

But instead, it was a plasticized card. Lowell froze.

On the card, clearly visible in the weak light of the streetlamp: ***BOOM. Next time it's for real.***

In the safety of the limo, Melinda held her father's hand. Andy had quickly left the glow of the TV in his Williamsburg loft to pick them up.

"Are you all right?"

"I'm fine, Dad, just a little shaken up."

"I hate to sound like a cliché, but at least we know we're on the right track. I need to talk to Roland first thing tomorrow. And to Johnny." He opened the refrigerator and took out two beers. "Beer all right with you?"

"Sure."

"Bermuda all right with you, too?"

Melinda laughed for the first time since they left the restaurant. "It's so true about men and boys and the price of their toys. How much did this cost you?"

"Not a penny. It was a gift from a grateful client."

He turned a few knobs and the windows darkened for a moment, and then lit up with the beaches of Bermuda slowly passing by on a beautiful summer's day. The sounds and smells that filled the limo were just what one would expect traveling through this tropical paradise.

They were quiet for a long time.

Melinda broke the silence. "My God, so who is threatening us?"

"There are many possibilities."

"But why?"

"We must be closer to the truth than we realize. You know," he proceeded carefully, "there is the possibility that our own client left the message."

Melinda stared at David.

He tried to ignore her, but finally looked her in the eyes. "I know you don't like to think about it, but it's still possible that she is guilty of murder, and if so, she could be capable of anything."

"And you think that she left that message to scare us off? How did she get out of the house without Julia noticing?"

"She did once before, remember?"

Melinda looked at her father and laughed out loud. "Oh, you old fool, don't you know she has a crush on you?"

"Yeah, right."

His daughter continued to laugh.

"You're serious, aren't you?"

She nodded. "You're the older man all little girls dream of. You're compassionate and understanding, you're smart as hell and you can take care of yourself. You make them feel safe and secure."

"I'm old enough to be..."

"That's exactly the point. You're old enough to be her father. Girls get tired of little boys, especially when they hit their thirties and their priorities change. Johnny had a lousy relationship with her father, so you've become the good daddy."

"Thank you, Carl Jung."

"I did minor in psychology, you know."

"I think she's a confused woman who only knows what she wants for the immediate moment."

"I agree. But I know what she wants right now, and that's you."

"So what would happen if she didn't get me?"

"That depends upon how severe her connection to you has become. If it's only a flirtation it should be harmless. But if it becomes an obsession she might have to act it out in some way."

"Like maybe trying to kill me?"

"I doubt it. More likely she would lie topless in your backyard and then unconsciously expose herself to you when you showed up."

"And if that didn't work, then would she try to kill me?"

Melinda didn't answer.

They sat back for a while and silently enjoyed the faux summer.

By the end of the ride, Lowell had made a major decision.

Chapter Twenty-One

The next morning, the whole crew was assembled at the townhouse. Melinda, Mort, Sarah, Julia, Andy, and Johnny sat around the living room on the couch or various chairs. Several suitcases stood out in the hallway by the bottom of the staircase.

Lowell stood by the fireplace. "As I told you all on the phone last night, from now on, this is the center of operation," he said. "Until we know what's going on, nobody is to leave here without Andy taking you."

He turned to Mort and Sarah.

"I don't know if you are targets as well, but you are all staying here until we can figure out what's going on. You'll both be well compensated for your time. Melinda, you can use the den for your office. Sarah, you and Mort will work downstairs in my office with me. Mort, would you please double-check the security now and then work on the hard drive some more. You got it from the office, yes?"

Mort nodded, his usual demeanor subdued after the news of last night.

"Julia, please prepare the guest rooms."

"What can I do?" asked Johnny.

"You can help me," said Julia.

Sarah fidgeted. "I've got a date tonight."

"I'm afraid you're going to have to cancel it," said Lowell.

"But he's a doctor."

"I'm sure he'll understand."

"Yeah, sure he will. I can just hear it now: Sorry I can't make it tonight, but someone is trying to blow me up. Would next week be convenient? Sure, he'll understand."

"I'm sorry Sarah, but it's for your own good. Now, can we get a little work done?"

Everyone got up to head to different parts of the house.

Lowell remained upstairs.

"Andy, can I see you for a minute?"

They went into the kitchen and Lowell closed the door.

"What's up, boss?"

"I want you to keep an eye on Johnny."

"Of course I will. I won't let anything happen to her."

"That's not exactly what I meant. I, uh, want you to watch her and let me know if she does anything out of the ordinary."

"Boss?"

"She is a strange woman, and until we know exactly what's going on here I want to be prepared for anything. Please don't mention this to anyone, especially Melinda."

Andy nodded.

"Oh, and Andy, when you go out would you mind stopping by the office and checking up on Buster and Keaton? Give them some food and maybe pet them a bit. They get lonely."

Andy smiled. "Sure boss, I'll take care of your friends. Hey, do you mind my asking, why turtles?"

"They live a long time."

"So?"

"I couldn't stand burying my dogs anymore."

Around ten, Lieutenant Roland and a plainclothes detective came by. The cop went downstairs to take a statement about last night from Melinda.

Roland got right to it. "Jesus Christ, who did you piss off? Who knew where you were going last night?"

"I don't know. I guess everyone at the house."

"Including Johnny Colbert?"

"Yes, including her."

"Has it occurred to you that your own client may have set up this thing?"

"Of course it's occurred to me. But you don't really think that, do you?"

"Why not? She may be a lot brighter than we think. She could have stabbed herself on Riker's just to get your attention so you would post bail. The wound wasn't life threatening and our investigation into that attack has turned up nothing. No witnesses, no suspects, nothing. Now maybe she figures if her lawyer gets scared off, she could get a mistrial and maybe aim our attention elsewhere. She has the ability to do this, and, since you bailed her out of jail, the opportunity."

"I don't think so," said Lowell, but his voice lacked conviction.

"Well, perhaps not, but someone got his hands on some powerful explosives and used it to blow up that judge."

"That doesn't mean that she did it."

"You think someone else got the explosives and waited until Johnny Colbert created a disturbance in court, and then killed Judge Winston?"

"Well, somebody killed her."

"Yes, your client."

"Or perhaps someone was waiting for an opportunity to kill the judge and when Johnny Colbert, an expert in demolition, had an altercation in her court, then they put the explosives in the judge's car."

"Just to pin it on your client? Even you can't believe that. To what end?"

"I don't know yet."

"That would have to be someone who had knowledge of the judge's calendar, and access to the explosives. You have someone in mind?"

"I'm not ready to point any fingers yet."

"I think you should revoke her bail and put her in jail where she belongs."

"I'm not going to do that. I'm still working a few angles."

"Okay," said Roland, "but if I were you I'd watch my back."

"That's my plan. We are all staying here. And you said on the phone that you've towed in my car and are going over it, just in case?

"Yup, we'll let you know. And we'll test that plastic greeting card, but I doubt we'll find anything, especially cause of the rain."

While everyone quietly had lunch at the dining room table, Lowell stayed at his desk. He pulled a drawer open and touched the cover of his ratty, as Melinda called it, ephemeris. He hoped to draw some energy, some clarity from its smooth cover.

Was Rosen less enamored with Judge Winston then he let on? Enough so to be involved in her death? Or could Lieutenant Roland possibly be right? Was Johnny responsible for all of it? Did she kill the judge? Inflict the wound on Riker's Island herself? Shred her own possessions and threaten to blow him up?

He closed the desk drawer, turned toward his computer, brought her chart up and tried to look at it from a fresh perspective, not as someone he had come to know.

It was time to learn a little more about their client.

Chapter Twenty-Two

"There's an old joke about a guy who walks into a bar and asks for a scotch on the rocks. The bartender puts the drink in front of him and says: *'That'll be four bucks.'* The guy gives him four singles. The bartender puts two in the register and two in his pocket. A little later the guy has another drink and again the bartender puts two singles in the register and two in his pocket. On the third round the bartender puts all four dollars in his pocket. The boss comes over and says: *What's the matter, we're not partners anymore?"*

"Are you implying that bartenders are not all honest?"

"Honest as the day is long. Unfortunately they work mostly at night." He barked out a laugh.

"Is Johnny honest?"

The owner stood behind the bar with a clipboard taking a liquor inventory. Lowell was on a stool, elbows uncomfortably up on the dark-wood countertop. The bar at three in the afternoon was otherwise empty. It struck him that the only thing sadder than a full bar was an empty one.

"Incredibly so. If one of her customers gets a load on and leaves her a lot of money, the next time that person comes in she gives it back to them and tells them to tip her now, while they're sober."

"How does that work out for her?'

"A few take the money back and leave a smaller amount. Most of them leave the original tip anyway. But boy, do they appreciate her honesty. Johnny wouldn't steal anything. If she finds a hundred dollar bill on the floor she'll wait at least a week to see if anyone claims it before spending it. How many people do you know would do that?"

"Is she good with her own money?"

"Not her own. She spends too much on silly stuff. Sometimes she's in debt and takes an advance on her salary. But hell, I don't mind."

"Still, you trust her."

"What do you think? This place is my whole life. Everything I have is here. She has keys to the restaurant, my private office, and even has access to the safe, in case I'm not around and there's an emergency. But Johnny's a hard girl to figure out. She's got a mouth that embarrasses cops and firemen, can have a short fuse, especially when she drinks. She's direct and honest, and expects the same from others. But you sure don't want to get on her bad side."

"Why is that?"

"Johnny's tough. She's been hurt a lot in her life and she knows how to hurt others. She can defend herself physically or verbally. And I've yet to see someone get the better of her when she has the truth on her side."

"Is the truth important to her?"

"More than anything. If you lie or cheat her or go behind her back she'll never forgive you. But you can say anything to her face and she'll take it."

"How long have you known her?"

"I met Johnny back in '90, I think, maybe '91. She had been in New York for about a year crashing on people's couches. I had a bartender I wanted to get rid of. Although I couldn't catch him, I knew he was a thief. But he was popular, and I was afraid I'd lose a lot of business if I let him go. One night Johnny walked in and sat at the bar. This guy started acting macho and giving her lip and she let him have it with both barrels. I mean, she chewed him a new one and made some of the regulars see for the first time what a jerk he really was. I liked her right away."

"When did she start working for you?"

"That very night. I fired him on the spot and the customers convinced me to put Johnny behind the bar. She needed a job, and I figured it wouldn't hurt to let her work out the night. The bar was slow, mostly regulars. They had to teach her how to make all the drinks. But they really seemed to like her. She learned fast and has been behind my bar ever since."

"So she has a temper," said Lowell.

"Oh, yes, but she usually only loses it if she's been drinking."

"You don't mind a bartender who drinks?"

"One Christmas someone gave me a beach towel that said: *Seeking honest, sober bartender. Will take either.* Drinking is a professional hazard in this business. I'd rather have a bartender who nips a little than one with sticky fingers."

"Tell me about her temper."

"Well, one time she hit a guy with a left hook. Knocked him clean off the stool."

"You didn't fire her for that?"

"Nope. She was right. He was a real asshole and kept harassing some women. She warned him several times, but he ignored her. Then he reached over the bar and grabbed her tits. That's when she slugged him. I helped throw the bum out."

"How about her social life?"

"Johnny? Ha. Her idea of a seductive line is: *Wanna fuck?"*

"Not subtle?"

"Usually if she's attracted to a guy at the bar, she just pours him free booze until he's snockered and then sticks her tongue down his throat."

"What if he doesn't respond the way she had hoped?'

"Then he'd better be wearing running shoes."

"Can she be vengeful?"

"Well, I, that is..."

"It's okay," said Lowell. "I'm on her side. I need to know everything I can about her."

"Well, yes. If you hurt Johnny she'll probably get you back. But it's always upfront and in your face. I don't think she could ever do what they said she did."

"So you would take her back after this murder business?"

"In a heartbeat. Are you kidding? The customers miss her. I can't hire anyone else until I know what her situation is. I'm tending bar during the day and put the day guy on at night. I hate it. He hates it. Christ, Johnny works twelve-hour shifts without as much as a complaint."

The chef stuck his head out of the kitchen. "Hey, Charlie, the meat never showed up today. I got a stew on the dinner menu I've got to prepare."

"All right, Marco, I'll call the butcher and see what's keeping it."

"Tough business," said Lowell.

"You don't know the half of it. There's always a million things to do, and never enough time to do them."

"So why do you stay in it?"

"I love the people."

Lowell nodded.

"Bet you haven't heard this one. A guy walks into an empty bar and orders a scotch on the rocks. The bartender says: 'I'm so glad you came in.' He points to a little black and white dog sitting on the bar. 'This talking dog wandered in an hour ago and it will answer any question you ask it.' 'Buddy, just give me my drink, will ya?' 'Wait,' says the bartender, 'I'll prove it.' He turns to the dog. 'What's on top of the house?' The dog says: 'Roof.' 'Buddy, give me my drink.' 'Wait, what's the opposite of smooth?' The dog says 'Ruff.' 'Look, I can go next door and get my drink.' 'Wait, just let me try once more. Who's the greatest baseball player who ever lived?' The dog says: 'Ruth.' 'That's it,' says that customer and he storms out. The dog looks at the bartender and says: 'DiMaggio?'"

Lowell chuckled.

"Where else can you hear jokes like that?"

"The borscht belt 1965?"

Charlie shrugged. "A good joke never gets old."

"Just one more question. How's business been?"

"Terrible. This has been the worst year since I opened the place in '85. If I didn't own the building I'd probably be closed by now, like so many other restaurants. But I've got an understanding landlord."

Lowell got up to leave and reached into his pocket. Charlie shook his head.

"You don't have to tip the owner. Just tell Johnny that we all miss her and wish her well. And let me know if there anything I can do to help."

Chapter Twenty-Three

"Something's wrong with this picture." Lowell held up the chart to Mort.

"What the problem?" Mort looked up from the second computer Lowell had brought in so Mort could work the hard drive full time.

It was a little before noon and they were in the downstairs office in the townhouse.

"The judge's clerk."

"Rosen?"

Lowell nodded. "He gave me his birth date as April 17, 1968."

"And you think that's wrong?"

"Let me give you a brief interpretation of the personality associated with this chart and you tell me if it sounds like the man you met the other day. This is an Aries Sun in trine to a Sagittarius Moon on one side and Jupiter on the other, creating a grand trine in fire. Mercury and Venus are also in Aries. This would be someone with a quick, open mind, an optimistic outlook and most likely, a more liberal attitude. It shows an active imagination that would continue to explore new ideas throughout his life. This person would also be apt to speak freely without hesitation and make decisions quickly."

Mort laughed. "That's certainly not the person I met."

"I know. Either he's a better actor than I think he is..."

"Or he lied about his birthday."

"I never gave it a second thought. There was no reason to doubt it. I mean why would he lie about something I could easily check? So I just assumed he had told me the truth. But the other day when we visited him, the chart just didn't jell. I've just been too busy to think about it. But I reexamined it last night."

"Don't you sleep?"

"I'll have plenty of time for that soon enough."

"Of course the question is why would he lie?"

"That's what we're going to find out. But first I need to know his real birth date."

"I'll get on it."

The phone rang. Lowell picked it up. "Starlight Detective Agency."

"Roland."

"Lieutenant, what can I do for you this morning?"

"It's more what I can do for you. I've got the report on the bomb that killed Judge Winston."

"What did they find?"

"It was a very sophisticated piece of equipment set off, as we assumed, by remote control."

"When you say *very sophisticated*, what do you mean?"

"The boys tell me the bomb itself was something that could only be put together by an expert. Whoever it was used Semtex, an older type of plastique explosive invented in the 1950s in the Czech Republic and first commercially manufactured in 1964. Apparently Semtex is the same product that was used in Pan Am103. The bomb and wiring were state of the art, but interestingly the detonation device was crude. Or rather, old-fashioned."

"Why would someone choose that particular type of explosive?"

"Because it is soft and malleable and works well in almost any temperature, making it safer and more versatile than other types that can be more temperamental."

"I see. Would you say this is something your everyday run-of-the-mill criminal would know about?"

"I doubt it. This stuff is primarily used in the military."

"Okay. Anything else?"

"They were able to trace the explosives. They were part of a shipment sold from a French firm to our military two years ago. We've been in touch with your client's commanding officer, a Colonel Eugene Marshal. He's ordered a complete inventory of supplies at the camp to see if anything is missing."

"Just one more question, Lieutenant. Could it have been set off via a cell phone?"

"I see you've met the charming Mr. Milford. Well, we thought of that ourselves, but according to our experts the detonator was too outdated for any digital device and had to be set off by someone right in the vicinity."

"Thank you, Lieutenant, I appreciate the call."

When he hung up Mort turned his chair around and dropped a piece of paper on Lowell's desk.

"The birth information of one Larry Rosen, compliments of Yearbook dot com. According to this he graduated from Glen Cove High School in 1987. They list his birthday as April 17th."

"That's the date he gave me," said Lowell.

"Ah," relied Mort, "but his year of birth is 1969, not 1968."

"Interesting. How reliable is this information?"

"It's on the Internet, so what do you think?"

"I think you better double-check it."

"I already did. He was born on Long Island at North Shore Hospital April 17, 1969, at 5:59 a.m., according to their records."

Lowell punched the revised birth data into his computer and picked up the new chart.

"This shows a much different person. There is a Sun – Saturn conjunct in Aries in the 12th House, which shows a restrictive and probably more conservative personality than Mr. Rosen's first chart. This aspect can be frustrating at times and tends to restrain and limit the person's growth, at least until middle age. Often there is a difficult relationship with the father. Mercury is in Taurus, a fixed sign, showing a slow and meticulous mind. Mercury conjuncts the Moon, which makes it rather difficult for him to separate his thoughts and emotions. And since the aspect is in a fixed sign he would be stubborn and inflexible, possibly even fanatical. Uranus conjuncts his South Node, which shows an explosive side to his personality that is usually kept hidden."

"That sounds like our boy."

"This chart also shows that he can be manipulated and easily frightened, which may prove to be useful information."

"So why did he lie?"

"Theoretically there could be dozens of reasons."

"Maybe," said Mort, "I bet he used that date since he was seventeen and bought his first phony I.D. so he could buy booze, and he got so used to quoting it that it just stuck in his mind."

"Why would you think of that?"

"Because that's what I did."

"Maybe, but I wouldn't bet on it. I believe there is only one reasonable explanation. I think that knowing I am an astrologer his instincts kicked in and he lied."

"Just to confuse you?"

Lowell nodded. "Misdirection is a powerful tool when used properly."

"It didn't work, did it?"

"Not for very long."

◇◇◇

That evening after dinner, Lowell asked to speak to Sarah for a moment.

"Tomorrow I want you to take Johnny to get her hair cleaned up and styled and then take her shopping for some new clothes. Andy will go with you. We need her to have a mature look for the jury."

Sarah's eyes lit up. "Sure! Everyone's having huge sales now. We'll go to Macy's and Bloomingdale's."

"Conservative outfits."

"Yes, boss."

"And Sarah,"

"Yes, boss?"

"Only one pair of shoes."

"Yes, boss," she said, with obvious disappointment.

Chapter Twenty-Four

It was ten the next morning and the New York State Thruway was fairly empty. They were moving along at a good pace.

"What would you like to look at?" Lowell swiveled on his bolted chair and reached to fiddle with a knob.

"How about the real thing?" It was sunny and the temperature was a balmy fifty degrees. Melinda opened the windows and let the fresh air fill the limo. "It's so beautiful up here this time of year." A little snow had stuck in the shade of the hills where the sun never hit. Lowell always marveled at how the landscape and weather could be so different so near such a large city.

"I suppose."

"Oh, dad, will you get your nose out of your damn work for just a minute and appreciate being alive?"

Lowell put the charts down. "All right, I'm looking."

Although the foliage was past its peak there were still occasional brilliant reds, yellows, and oranges passing by. Lowell took a deep breath and absorbed the scenery. "I hope this trip isn't a waste of time."

"I had to depose Colonel Marshal anyway," said Melinda.

"You could have done it on Skype."

"I know, but this is an opportunity for you to look around."

"And for you to get out of the office for an afternoon."

"There's that."

They exited the thruway at the foothills of the Catskill Mountains and headed up into the back country, passing through several small towns, all displaying signs welcoming the men and women in uniform.

The army camp was situated down a long road cut deep into the woods. Except for the fences lining the side of the road and an occasional *no trespassing* sign, there was nothing to denote this as anything more than a sleepy country byway, until they came to a gatehouse and a soldier in uniform. The limo was stopped at the gate, a phone call was made, and they were ushered into the camp. The colonel was waiting for them outside his headquarters.

"Would you mind if we walked around the compound while we talked?" asked Colonel Marshal.

"Not at all," said Melinda.

He was wearing a light brown topcoat casual uniform, and his walk was stiff and purposeful, like one would expect of a career military man. The site was much larger than it first appeared. They strolled slowly through the compound past the barracks.

Lowell followed the two at a few paces. He stroked his ponytail once and looked about as they walked. He didn't love things military.

Melinda turned on her portable recorder. "Would you tell us a little bit about Johnny Colbert?"

"Private Colbert can be a pain in the ass," said the colonel. "She always has to do things her way, and it makes for some difficult moments."

"And how long has she been in the reserves?"

"Three years."

"So she was almost thirty-seven when she signed on. Wasn't that a little old to be joining up?"

"I suppose so, but you should have seen the fight in her. She took out women and men twice her size. Could run the obstacle course in record time, and was smart as a whip."

"How was her discipline?"

"Well, discipline was not her strongest suit."

"Was she a problem?"

"She wasn't a problem; just had her own way of going about things."

"She didn't like rules, is that it?"

"You've met her. What do you think?"

"Any trouble with alcohol?"

"Absolutely not. Whatever our reservists do in their off time is their business, but when they are under my command, I demand a clear head. No booze and no drugs. Besides, Johnny took her time here very seriously. She was always sober and conscientious. I never saw or heard of her even having a social drink while in camp."

"And her specialty?"

"All types of explosives."

"Isn't that a bit of a broad subject?"

"When she first joined us, she showed a great interest and aptitude for them. She studied with our trainers and learned all they could teach her. Then she went off and studied the subject on her own. She would sit in front of the computer for hours researching any new inventions that came along and trying to stay on top of things. By the end of her second year with us, there wasn't any conventional bomb she didn't know how to build, detonate, or dismantle, sometimes under direct fire."

"Isn't it true that at the request of the New York police department you took an inventory of the explosives in your unit?"

"Yes ma'am, that is true."

"And what did you find?"

"There was a substantial amount of one type of explosive missing."

"And what type is that?"

"Semtex."

"The same type of explosives used in the bomb that killed Judge Winston. After discovering that the explosives were missing what did you do?"

"I reported it to my superiors and gave a copy of the report to the New York City police."

"Had Johnny been on active duty in the previous period before the explosives went missing?"

"Yes, she had been in camp about a week before."

"And being one of your main experts on explosives, did she have access to them?"

"Yes."

"Do you think she could have built and detonated the type of bomb used to kill Judge Winston?"

"Well, I, that is..."

Melinda turned off the recorder. "Colonel, we're here to help Johnny, not hang her. That's the district attorney's job. I have to consider everything the state will bring up and be prepared for it. Just tell us the truth. We'll sort it out later."

"I understand."

She turned the device back on.

"Yes, Johnny could have built the bomb."

"Isn't it true that Johnny Colbert received the highest commendation awarded in the peacetime reserves?"

"That is correct. She risked her life under fire to dismantle a bomb that had been planted by the enemy."

"She saw combat?" asked Lowell, incredulously.

"Well, domestic combat. We got into a skirmish with Justice Corps, one of those survivalist groups based further upstate. Somehow they got into our camp and put a bomb under one of the barracks and trapped twenty-three men and women inside. Then they tried to hold us off with semi-automatics until the timer could detonate. Johnny ran right in the middle of the battle and dismantled it. Saved a lot of lives too. As far as I'm concerned, Johnny Colbert is a hero."

"Okay," said Melinda, "we'll see if we can figure out how you can say that on the witness stand."

They passed a group of men and women doing calisthenics.

"Isn't it true," continued Melinda, "that the explosives found missing from your camp could have been taken at anytime over the previous month?"

"Yes. I'm sorry to say that there was a lapse in security that only required us to account once a month for some of the rarely used munitions. In large part because of this case, the army is in the process of correcting that oversight. And since the theft was only discovered in the inventory taken at the end of the monthly cycle, it could have been removed anytime within the previous thirty days."

"Perhaps even the day before the murder?"

"Yes, that is possible, although it would be difficult for someone without clearance to get into camp."

"Justice Corps managed to."

The colonel nodded grimly.

"How many people are there permanently placed in the explosives unit?"

"Seventeen."

"And how many of them have the knowledge to produce a bomb such as the one used to kill Judge Winston?"

The Colonel thought for a moment. "I would say five."

"And how many of those five people live in New York City and would likely have had knowledge of Judge Winston?"

"I don't know. I'd have to look that up."

"Let me save you the trouble," said Melinda, with a heavy sigh. "The answer is one. Johnny Colbert."

Chapter Twenty-Five

Lowell and Melinda had just gotten back from their sojourn upstate when Sarah and Johnny returned from their shopping spree. Johnny was dressed in a dark blue, conservative business outfit with a jacket, slacks, and white buttoned-up blouse that hid all traces of her tattoo. Her hair had been trimmed and styled, with a flip over one eye. She wore a little makeup, just lipstick and some foundation to add color to her cheeks. But it made a major difference in her appearance. She looked more like a Wall Street yuppie than the hard-drinking, foul-mouthed terror Melinda had met on Riker's only weeks before. When she saw herself in the dining room mirror she laughed out loud.

"My mother wouldn't recognize me."

"Johnny," said Melinda, "why, you're very beautiful."

"Ah, I am not."

"Sarah, you did a great job."

"Yeah, it was cool, like *My Fair Lady*. And just one pair of shoes, per instructions," with a wink at Lowell.

Lowell was beaming. "You look terrific."

Johnny blushed. "I guess a new outfit and a little paint can do wonders."

"You've got to have something to work with first, or all the window dressing won't make any difference."

She smiled. "I guess so. But shopping with Sarah was a real education. God, you should have heard her talking to the sales people. She knows more about clothes and shoes than anyone I ever knew. She was telling them things about the stuff they were selling that none of them knew. She should be in the business."

"Maybe she will be one day. For now I need her to run my office, so please don't give her any ideas."

◇◇◇

An hour later Lowell came down the basement stairs just as he heard Melinda click a cellphone closed and let out a groan. "They're going to start with jury selections next week."

"When you get the list of perspective jurors, bring it to me," said Lowell, "along with their birth information, if possible."

"I want to see how you do this. Vetting a jury is a complicated psychological process that can ultimately win or lose a case."

"That's why I want to study their birth charts and be sure we have a good group to work with."

"I understand that some attorneys spent a fortune trying to get that information," said Sarah. "You can get it from a birth chart?"

"I believe so."

"How?"

"The chart gives me their basic psychological makeup. It will help us choose those that are most open-minded and fair. We're going to be discussing some issues that are quite foreign to most of these people, such as astrology."

"Will it work?" asked Sarah.

"It will at least give us a fighting chance. Remember, we only have to have one vote for acquittal to have a hung jury."

"Well," said Melinda, "we'd better find something to build a defense on or it won't matter much. They fast-tracked this case for a reason. They're not interested in justice. I think they just want this all to go away."

◇◇◇

Later that evening, after a wonderful dinner prepared by Julia, everyone went in different directions in the increasingly claustrophobic townhouse.

Lowell and Johnny headed for the TV room. Johnny flipped channels until she stopped just as the local news was ending.

"Good evening and welcome to the New York State Lottery. I'm Yolanda Vega. And now, here is tonight's numbers."

Johnny reached into her back pocket and took a wad of lottery tickets out and held them up. When the numbers had been drawn she threw them on the table in disgust.

"When did you get a chance to buy those?" asked Lowell.

"When we were out shopping."

Lowell said nothing.

"I felt lucky."

"Lucky? You're on trial for first-degree murder, you've been stabbed, and most of your possessions have been destroyed. Why would you feel lucky?"

"I saw my birthday on two different license plates, so I had to play it."

"Why do you buy these awful things?"

"Because."

"Because why?"

She shrugged.

"Don't you know that the odds of winning anything worthwhile are astronomical?"

"I guess."

"So why?"

"Because."

Lowell waited.

"I get up at noon, exercise, run a few errands and then it's time to go to work until three in the morning, where I spend most of my life entertaining drunks and people that couldn't give a crap about me. Outside of my co-workers I have very few friends, no steady boyfriend, and no family."

She sipped her drink.

"I haven't been to the movies in two years. Except for drinking and eating out, there's nothing that I enjoy."

"But don't you feel foolish when you buy them?"

"At least..." she stopped.

"At least what?"

"At least I feel something."

Chapter Twenty-Six

Lowell was up early with hot coffee by his side. Time was running out. The evidence was overwhelming, and if he couldn't solve this thing before the trial started, Johnny's prospects didn't look too good. His desk was inundated with astrology charts scattered haphazardly.

Melinda and Sarah came in, each with her hands around a ceramic mug of morning gold. A chill had hit the city during the night and the townhouse's heat was just kicking in.

Lowell turned to the astrology computer program. "It's time to try something new." He hit the *now* button which brought a chart onto the screen. "Who is responsible for the death of Farrah Winston?"

"What are you doing?" asked Melinda.

"It's a horary chart."

"What's a *whore airy* chart?" asked Sarah.

"Horary," said Lowell, "it means *of the hour*."

"How does it work?"

"A single question is posed and should be answerable through the position of the planets exactly when the question is asked."

"Didn't you ask two questions?"

"Not really. What I am seeking is the solution to the question of who committed the murder."

He printed the chart.

"What does it say?" Melinda was looking over his shoulder.

"What do you think?"

"We never spent much time on horary work. You always said it would just add to my obsession with boys and I'd appreciate it more when I was older."

"Was I wrong?"

Melinda shrugged. "Probably not."

"You had a lot of boyfriends?" asked Sarah.

Lowell laughed. "You should have seen her when she was younger. Sometimes she would juggle three at once."

"I've grown up," said Melinda.

"Well, maybe it's curable," replied the redhead.

"Anyway," continued Lowell, "the ascendant of this chart is two degrees, which means that there isn't enough information yet to get a definitive answer. But it may still reveal something that will prove useful." He tugged on his ponytail as he studied the chart. "The ruler of the ascendant is in the 3rd House conjunct the North Node, and it has just completed a square to Neptune. Clearly this is speaking about distraction and misdirection. Perhaps some paperwork of some sort holds the key. The answer is in the detail." He sipped his coffee. "Someone very close to her had a hand in this. Someone she had dealings with on a daily basis."

"The 3rd House also rules siblings," said Melinda. "Maybe her sister had something to do with it?"

"Yes, possibly. They seemed to have a strained relationship, and their charts are anything but passive. Also, the sister's husband is unemployed and their money problems will be solved for now with her inheritance. I have not ruled her out."

He pinned the chart to his bulletin board and sat back. "Where's Mort?"

"Upstairs somewhere," said Sarah.

"Find him, will you?"

"Yes, boss." She went up the stairs.

Melinda looked worried.

"Try not to fret," said Lowell. "We may be closer than we think."

Mort entered the office. "You're looking for me?"

"I want you to follow some minor leads. We're missing something, something small and seemingly insignificant."

"The devil is in the details, isn't that what they say?"

"And here's the proof of that saying. How are you coming with that hard drive?"

"I got through some of the defenses. Here are the file names I've been able to extract so far. Nothing dramatic or I would've called you in the car yesterday"

He handed Lowell a folder holding several sheets of paper. Lowell glanced quickly through it.

"Doesn't seem to be much here. Mostly financial records and what looks like some court business. Hardly worth hiding behind so elaborate a defense system." He picked up a pen and circled several entries, and then handed the folder back to Mort. "What do you think these stand for?"

"P.C." read Mort. "Don't know. Maybe someone's initials?"

"They show up quite a number of times. Maybe they're connected. I think you should start there."

"Already have," said Mort, with his impish grin. "I thought you might suggest that."

"So what's next?" asked Melinda.

"Let's look at Larry Rosen's chart again," said Lowell. He worked the computer for a few minutes. "The corrected birth information for Rosen shows a personality much more capable of subterfuge and underhanded actions. I might have missed the deception had I not been aware of the discrepancies."

"Mistakes in astrology?" asked Mort.

Lowell shook his head. "Astrology never makes mistakes. Astrologers on the other hand…"

He worked the computer for a few more minutes.

"What about his relationship with Judge Winston?" asked Melinda.

"This composite chart of Rosen and Farrah Winston is also much different than the one I drew with his wrong birth information. There is a Sun Venus conjunct in a tight square to Pluto. It clearly shows some hidden agenda and the deterioration of their relationship."

"So you were right," said Mort. "Rosen must have given you the wrong information on purpose."

"I suppose so. There was a powerful connection between them that one would expect. After all, he was her clerk and close associate for several years. But there was more going on than could be seen on the surface."

"Can you tell what it is?"

"It had a lot to do with their philosophies on life. The ruler of the composite 9th House sits on the ascendant. I'll need to work with this for a while. I'll do it later tonight."

"And now?" asked Melinda.

"Now we push and pull until the pieces fall into place and the jigsaw reveals its picture. Mort, let me know when you open some of these P.C. files."

"All right. What are you going to do?"

"Gaze upon my grand estate."

Mort laughed. "If you get lost, I'll send out the hounds."

Lowell went into the back room and sat in his armchair looking out the window at his tiny patch of land. Melinda followed a few moments later.

"What are you thinking about?" she asked.

"Oh, just remembering the years of struggle and frustration, with little fondness, I might add. I guess I'm still a bit amazed at my success."

"You don't seem like a rich man. You don't feel settled or comfortable at all. Money is supposed to make someone content, at the very least. You somehow seem even more displaced as the years go on."

A sycamore hung over his property from the next, the branches swayed slightly in the brisk autumn wind. Lowell stood up, opened the window and breathed in a jolt of cool air. Then he sat back in the chair.

"Don't forget, I was almost fifty when I finally started making a decent income. Before that, the time and effort wasted scampering for rent and food was trivial and counterproductive."

"I thought struggle strengthens us?"

"Perhaps in youth. In middle years it only wears you down and steals your faith. In fact, my real work only began when my fortunes improved. Now maybe I can make a tiny difference. What I see happening around me in our society becomes more disturbing as time goes on. How could I relax once I had money?"

They continued to look out the window.

"I remember how beautiful it was here last year when it snowed. I spent a long weekend with my college roommate, Jill, during that blizzard in January. We built a snowman and you built a fire and Julia just spoiled us terribly. I think I gained ten pounds in four days. But it was so nice to have that feeling of being in a home, with a private backyard right in the middle of the city. I felt like I was ten again."

He nodded. "I hope we have many snowy days here for years to come."

He paused.

"Maybe you'll even bring your children."

Melinda laughed. "Took you long enough to get to that one."

Mort entered and cleared his throat. They turned from the window.

"I think I found something interesting."

"Do tell."

"I opened one of the files marked P.C."

Mort handed Lowell a legal size piece of paper upon which was some sort of diagram.

"What is this?"

"That is a blueprint of some sort."

Lowell looked at it for a few moments. "I don't know what I'm looking at."

Mort shook his head. "Neither do I."

"Obviously it's the outline of some sort of complex; there are some buildings and this looks like a road."

"Maybe this is something our elusive P.C. was working on," said Melinda.

"Maybe. Mort, run through the judge's records and see if anyone with those initials comes up. And keep working on those other files. We must find out who this P.C. is and what he or she had to do with the victim."

Melinda's cell phone rang. She left the room.

She returned a few minutes later.

"Well, that was interesting."

Chapter Twenty-Seven

"Judge Thompson called."

"The same Judge Thompson who is presiding over Johnny's murder trial?"

"He wants to see me in his chambers at 11:30."

"So?"

"With you."

"Me?"

"Yep."

"That *is* interesting."

"I assume this meeting has to do with my name being on your witness list."

"I suppose so. We'll find out soon enough."

Johnny came into the room. "I'm getting a little, you know, stir-crazy."

"If you want to, you can come with us to the courthouse and wait in the limo with Andy," said Lowell.

"Yeah, anything. Just so long as I get out of here for a little while."

Andy pulled up in front of the courthouse and watched vigilantly as Melinda and her father walked up the steps. Johnny stayed in the back and watched TV.

They took the elevator to the fourth floor and were ushered into the judge's chambers, where they were met by Judge Thompson and Greg Harris, the prosecuting attorney.

"Ms. Lowell," said the judge, "I've called this meeting at the request of Mr. Harris. He has some questions regarding Mr. Lowell's name on your witness list. Could you elaborate a bit?"

"Certainly. I intend to call David Lowell to the stand."

"But in what capacity?" interjected Harris. "Is Mr. Lowell testifying as a private detective or as an astrologer?"

"Ms. Lowell?" asked the judge.

"As both, your honor."

"Then I strongly object," said Harris. "Are we going to bring up psychics and palm readers next?"

"Precedent has been set," said Melinda,

"It has?" asked the judge.

"Yes, your honor, it's all in my brief." She handed the judge a file. "I refer to New York Criminal Reports, Volume 32, *The People vs. Evangeline Adams*. You will find the references right there."

Judge Thompson picked up the papers and glanced at them. "Are you familiar with this case?" he asked Harris.

The prosecutor shook his head. "No, I'm not."

"I took the liberty of printing a copy for you as well." She handed him a file.

"Well," said the judge, "since it's almost lunch time, let's reconvene at one o'clock. I'll take a look at this and give you my decision at that time."

Lowell and Melinda stopped by the limo and picked up their client, and then hurried to a nearby restaurant to grab a quick lunch. When they were seated Melinda spoke.

"Do you think he'll accept the Evangeline Adams case as precedent?"

"You know the law better than I, what do you think?"

Melinda just shrugged. "I think it's fifty-fifty."

"Who is Evangeline Adams?" asked Johnny.

Melinda was perusing the menu. "She was an influential astrologer in the early part of the twentieth century. She had her own radio show and had many important clients, including J.P. Morgan and other wealthy financiers. Evangeline Adams was arrested and put on trial in 1914 for fortune-telling, which is against the law in New York State."

"What happened?"

"Well, she demanded that they put astrology itself on trial to prove that it was not fortune-telling, but rather a well studied and respected science. By explaining how it works, she successfully convinced the court that astrology was in fact a science and was acquitted of all charges. She went on to predict many future events, some that she did not live to see, including the stock market crash of 1929 and the Second World War."

"But then, she was a fortune teller, wasn't she?"

"What she proved in court was that knowing the position of the planets and interpreting their *potential* results is quite different than stating for a fact that something will happen. What she was able to do in life was predict quite a number of important events. And yes, frankly I would call that fortune-telling."

"Can he," she nodded toward Lowell, "predict things like that?"

"Oh, yes. My father has written of many world events well in advance. You'll probably hear about some of them if he gets on the stand."

"So what happens now?"

"That depends upon the judge," said Melinda. "If he agrees with the argument set out in my brief, he will have to allow my father to testify."

"And if not?"

"Then we will have to find another way of introducing any evidence we uncover."

Lowell glanced at his watch. "Okay, let's get back there."

◇◇◇

"All right, Ms. Lowell," said the judge, "I've read your brief on *The People vs. Evangeline Adams*. After serious consideration and with some trepidation I will allow into evidence the testimony of Mr. Lowell. But I reserve the right to stop this examination if it gets too far out of line. Do I make myself clear?"

Melinda and Lowell both nodded.

"Your honor," said the prosecutor, "I must strongly voice my objections to this entire procedure. This is simply silly; there's no other word for it. We are modern, enlightened people, living in the twenty-first century." He turned to Lowell. "This nonsense belongs in the middle ages with pagan rituals and witches. There is no scientific foundation for the belief in astrology. It is used to dupe the simple-minded and create self-fulfilling prophesies."

"Objection noted," said the judge. "You'll have your chance in cross-examination. Now let's get on with this, shall we?"

"By the way, I've looked at your chart, Mr. Harris," said Lowell.

"I'm not interested in that drivel."

Lowell nodded. "I understand. It's just foolishness."

"That's right."

"By the way, how's that diabetes?"

"It's much better," said Harris. "It only bothers me when my blood sugar is…your honor!"

"Mr. Lowell," said the judge, "please."

Chapter Twenty-Eight

After leaving the judge's chambers, Lowell, Johnny, and Melinda were in the limo when the phone rang.

"Are you on the way back to the townhouse?" asked Mort.

"Why, what's up?"

"I managed to open another of the files titled P.C. I think you'd like to see it."

"Ah, and do you know who our elusive P.C. is?"

"It's not a who. It's a what."

"We're on our way."

He turned off the speakerphone. "Andy?"

"I heard."

Mort held a single piece of paper. "P.C. stands for Pilgrim's Cavern, a small town in Utah. It's so small it isn't even on maps or on the state's website. I've gone through the usual searches, but so far I haven't been able to get much information at all. It's almost as if it never existed."

"Isn't that a little strange?" asked Melinda.

"Not really," replied Mort. "If a town is small enough or just wishes anonymity it might be able to avoid the prying eyes of our compulsively curious society. Someone has to bother to enter the data into a computer bank for it to show up. Maybe nobody thought it was important enough to do so."

"Or maybe they just didn't want to be bothered by the outside world," she said.

"If so," replied Mort, "it looks like that will no longer be the case."

"What do you mean?"

Lowell answered. "Whatever the ultimate outcome of this, Pilgrim's Cavern will most likely get more publicity than it ever dreamed of."

"Or wanted, I'm sure," replied Melinda.

"In fact," said Mort, "there is so little data in the file I opened that I'm surprised Judge Winston even bothered to encrypt it. It just gives the town's name and location, and mentions something called P.D.I. I don't know what that stands for, but I'll follow up on it."

"Obviously she was taking extreme measures to protect a secret of some sort. So that's the diagram we were looking at the other day?" said Lowell.

"I would guess so," said Mort.

"That didn't look like the outline of an old town."

"I know. So far I can't even get any background information. I'll do a little surfing this afternoon. There are still two files marked P.C. that I have to open. I hope they will enlighten us some more."

"Okay, so what has this town in Utah have to do with our case?"

"I don't know. You're the detective. Detect something."

Lowell turned to his computer screen and typed feverishly for about fifteen minutes. "According to Google, Utah State Senator Smith dropped dead recently."

"Is that right?" Melinda nodded as she digested this news.

"Just about a month or so before Judge Winston was murdered."

"What are you thinking?"

Lowell opened a file and took out the victim's astrology chart. "Farrah Winston was born on August 26, 1976, in a suburb of

Salt Lake City, Utah. Did Rosen tell us that she was about to move back to Utah?"

Mort nodded. "That's right."

"What does that mean?" asked Melinda.

"I don't know. But at least we have a direction. All right, Mort, get me anything you can about Pilgrim's Cavern, Utah, the late Senator Smith, and any connection between the two and the victim."

"Will do."

"And keep working with that hard drive. I think it holds many more secrets."

"But just like the women in my life, it has no intention of giving them up without a struggle."

"Well," said Lowell, "let the seduction begin."

Chapter Twenty-Nine

Lowell was putting in his morning trades. "Roger, tell me what you know about real estate."

"In what capacity?" Roger's voice squawked over the speaker phone.

"I'm looking into big land deals in a specific area of the U.S."

"Oh, so you've finally gotten that rich, huh?"

"It has to do with a case I'm working on."

"Well, I'm having lunch in The World Financial Center with George Morris from Goodman, Roth and Morris today. He's the best real estate lawyer I know. Why not join us? It'll finally get you down here. Besides, he'll be able to answer any questions you have."

"Well, I…"

"Good, then it's settled."

Melinda and Johnny had to make a brief early-morning appearance at the courthouse. Just some pretrial formalities. Andy drove them down.

"I'm hungry," said Johnny. "I didn't eat before we left."

Melinda opened the minirefrigerator. "There's some juice, carrots, a few cookies and some yogurt."

Johnny wrinkled her nose.

Melinda handed her a yogurt and a spoon. "Here, start with this."

Johnny reluctantly took the offering. She opened it and sniffed, scooping a bit out. "Hey," she said, eating just what was on the tip of the spoon, "I don't mean to pry, but like your old man's really rich." She ate the rest of what was on the utensil and dipped it again.

"Yes," said Melinda, matter-of-factly, "he's quite well-off."

"We talked about some of it. He bought oil futures and made a fortune."

"That's right."

"He's very smart, huh?"

"Yes, he is."

"He and your mom divorced?"

"Uh huh."

Johnny dipped her spoon in and twirled it, mixing the fruit and the yogurt together. She licked the spoon catlike, reaching her tongue around it rather than turning it. "Does he date anyone?"

Melinda laughed. "To tell you the truth, I really don't know. It's not something we talk about."

"Oh." She ate another spoonful of yogurt and pointed at the control panel. "What are all these gadgets?"

"This is his office on wheels. Everything he needs to do his work is here, so please don't touch anything."

"I wasn't going to." She scowled. "I'm not stupid, you know. I just didn't have the education you had."

"I didn't mean to imply…"

Johnny held up her hand. "That's all right. I'm a little touchy these days, that's all. And I'm nervous, that's all… oh damn it."

"What's the matter?"

"When I get nervous I start to repeat a phrase over and over again and I can't stop myself, that's all. See? I did it again, that's all, that's all, that's all…" She physically held her mouth shut with her hands.

"Try not to worry. I believe you're innocent, and my father will help me prove it. Now try to relax."

"How can I?"

Melinda raised the windows and started fiddling with the knobs on the console. "This might help. What's your favorite place in the world?"

"The ocean. I wish I were there now."

"Ever been to California?"

"Yeah, twice. I loved it, especially the coastline."

"Well, sit back and just relax. Andy, could we take a little ride?"

"Sure." He raised the glass barrier to maximize the effects of the system.

Melinda hit the ON button and the windows darkened for a moment. Then they lit up with the scene of a perfect day on the California coastal highway, she heard Johnny utter a very subdued "Wow."

Then there was silence.

Andy brought Johnny into Lowell's office. "I dropped Melinda off at her office. I'm going up to the kitchen for some of Julia's amazing coffee."

Johnny smiled at Lowell. "That's some car you got. Those windows are amazing."

Lowell was watching a muted CNN. "You like it, huh?"

"Yeah, it's fuck…

Lowell frowned.

"…freaking cool."

"Yeah, I guess it is."

"You don't like when I curse?"

"Not really."

"Why?"

"Well, for one thing it weakens you. Most people don't hear what you say, only how you say it. There are times when we must use harsh language for effect or perhaps as a defense. Cursing inappropriately shows a lack of control, and that can frighten someone. When you scare people, they are less likely to take you seriously, except as a threat."

"I never thought of it that way."

"Besides, it's not really who you are."

"What do you mean?"

"You weren't always this angry woman you've become. I assume it's the circumstances you have dealt with that have hardened your personality and forced you to build walls. You don't trust people, so you act in ways that will push them away. Most people have probably hurt you or let you down. This way you keep them at bay so you won't be hurt again."

Johnny thought about it. "I don't know about all that," she replied, "but I'll try not to curse anymore. At least around you. Okay?"

"Thank you, Johnny. I'm off for a lunch meeting. Think about what I said about what you say and how to use it as a strength, not a weakness."

Chapter Thirty

Lowell would have preferred to take the subway to Lower Manhattan alone, but until he knew who was stalking him he was force to acquiesce and had Andy drive him to Church Street. Once there, however, he insisted on walking toward the river by himself. Andy would be nearby but this was one trip he felt he had to make alone. It had been years since he came down here, and he needed the chance to stroll through his old stomping grounds and maybe bury an errant ghost or two.

For ten years he had worked in 2 World Trade Center on the floor of the Mercantile Exchange, the last five while living in Battery Park City after his divorce. He was at work on 9/10. Just because of circumstances, he was uptown on 9/11.

Everything seemed so different. This part of lower Broadway used to be inundated with commodities brokers, back room desk traders, and hedge fund operators. In those days lunch time on Liberty Street was a hectic flood of trading badges and harried capitalists scurrying to grab a sandwich before the afternoon trading session. Now it was a trickle of local workers. The tension that surrounded this neighborhood like a dust cloud was gone. But what was in its place was far more disconcerting.

It was when he crossed Church Street and started climbing the makeshift staircase that it really hit him. It wasn't exactly nostalgia. Those years of struggle didn't warrant such a response. It was more just sadness of a profound and universal kind. Finally, at least they were rebuilding.

He walked through the pathway that ran some thirty feet above West Street, connecting this tiny neighborhood built on landfill like a Band-Aid with the rest of Manhattan. He took the escalator down to street level. Battery Park City had grown radically since he'd moved out. The building expansion over the past decade had more than doubled the population. He entered The World Financial Center and walked to the Chinese restaurant.

They were already seated when Lowell arrived.

"David Lowell," said Roger, "George Morris."

"Nice to meet you," said Morris.

"Nice of you to invite me. I've been meaning to come down for some time."

"Let's order first," said Roger. "They get very busy at lunchtime."

The waiter took the order.

"Did you work down here?" asked Morris.

Lowell nodded. "On the floor of the old Merc."

"So Roger says you have some questions regarding real estate deals. How can I help you?"

"Ever hear of Pilgrim's Cavern?"

"No, what is it?"

Lowell took out the blueprint and laid it across the table. "Tell me what I'm looking at."

Morris look at it for a few minutes, uttering an occasional "hmm" or "well, well." Finally he looked at Lowell.

"Here," Morris pointed to the paper, "is a heliport, and here a small landing strip, probably for private planes. It doesn't look big enough for commercial airliners. This is the symbol for a hotel, and this is an apartment complex, complete with indoor and outdoor pools, tennis courts and a golf course. This appears to be situated up in the mountains somewhere on a plateau. There is one road in and out. As the name implies, there is a cavern, or more correctly a series of caverns. The caverns themselves are divided into what I believe are storage units, living spaces, and common areas. There is even a cave set aside for livestock, as this rather crude drawing of a cow would attest, though how they would graze them I don't know."

He picked up his tea and took a sip. "What you are looking at is a gold-plated, first-class Noah's Ark."

"That's about what I figured," said Lowell.

"This isn't the first blueprint of one of these I've seen, but it certainly is the most elaborate. These guys are what we call blueblood survivalists."

"Name sort of tells it all, huh?"

"That's about the size of it."

"So what does this all mean?"

"We are in the middle of the largest land grab since the government gave you seven acres and a mule just for the asking."

"What kind of land grab? We're at in a deep recession. I thought real estate was dead."

"Suburban houses and beach front condos aren't selling. I'm talking about huge chunks of America up for grabs. This has been going on for decades, but it really took off after 9/11. And since the crash of '08 this sort of thing has been escalating quickly. First of all, states are scrambling to get money anywhere they can before the whole thing falls to crap. They have to pay cops and firemen, and keep the buses running and sewers working. So they're looking at anyone who still has any money. And believe me, a lot of people do. There's more money around now than ever before in man's history, even with the collapse of the equity markets. This country isn't going out of business; it's just redefining who owns what."

"All right, so there are a lot of wealthy people out there."

"And all of them just as scared as the guy living in one room above a deli. There are more and more gated communities with private security forces that could qualify as militias. What with the fears of global warming, social breakdown, riots, nuclear bombs and God knows what else, the rich are purchasing huge chunks of land all over the place. Hollywood stars may own a house in Beverly Hills, but they also have property in Colorado, or Oregon, or freaking Kansas. Nobody trusts the coasts anymore. The richer ones have self-sustaining ranches with generators, huge rooms for stock piling, and security."

"Sounds a bit paranoid."

"You don't know the half of it," said Morris, pointing to the blueprint. "Okay, see this is what I'm talking about. This is set up as a gigantic upper-class survival camp. This sort of thing is going on all over the country, in fact all over the world. But I've got to tell you, this one makes the others I've seen pale in comparison."

"How deep do these caverns go?"

"There's no way to tell from these diagrams, but I would guess several miles."

"So these people are playing for keeps."

"This is a self-contained bit of humanity that could number a thousand families or more and probably would survive a nuclear war."

"How much would something like this cost?"

"Hard to tell, but well in the billions. The buy-in price could be quite high, maybe as much as a hundred million each."

Roger had been listening intently. "Quite a high-priced country club."

"Maybe, but it offers more than just golf and swimming. It offers survival."

Chapter Thirty-One

"Once you pointed me in the right direction," said Mort, "I was able to access some obscure state files."

The last of the day's sun was disappearing out the windows of the townhouse office.

"And what did you find out?"

"Just like that lawyer said. Pilgrim's Cavern is situated on a plateau up in the mountains. There's a single road leading in and out, making it fairly inaccessible, except by that road or by helicopter."

"What did you learn about the place?"

"The town was settled in 1895 by a group of disgruntled people from Salt Lake City. They had grown discontented with the encroaching secular world and found the isolation to their liking, so they went about building a small, isolated community."

"Isolated is right."

"As the name implies, the town was built near a cavern that is connected into a series of other caverns and caves that extends for miles deep into the mountainside. There's a fresh-water lake nearby and streams that run through the area, and they were able to produce enough food to survive. There are currently 865 people living there."

"Go on."

"About three years ago a financial group, Purple Diamond Industries, or P.D.I., submitted plans to buy the town and turn it into an escape for the very wealthy. The plans included a four-star hotel and sporting center with year-round indoor and outdoor sports. It was to be a retreat of the highest caliber, catering only to the elite. Eventually there would be several condo complexes built with prices beginning in the millions. It is quietly being touted as a first-class safe haven with natural protection against any kind of geopolitical disaster."

"Roger's friend was right on the money."

"So it would seem."

"Okay, what else did you learn?"

"The Pilgrim's Cavern project was all set to begin this spring. It was expected to take five years to complete, with construction costs priced at between five and six billion dollars."

"A bunch of that would have found its way into the state budget, I suppose. Motivation enough. You said it *was* all set to begin."

"That's right. Most of the lawsuits had been settled or pushed out of the way, and they were just about to award construction contracts."

"So, what happened?"

"As you noted the other day, State Senator Smith had the misfortune to drop dead of a massive coronary before the state legislature had a chance to vote on finalizing the project. Apparently it was a fiercely contested venture with a single swing vote in favor. Various groups, including environmentalists, had lobbied hard against it. If they don't vote the project in by the first of January, it will go into committee for another year where it may very well die. The governor, who is a Republican, had to pick someone for the open seat."

"Interesting," said Lowell.

"You'll never guess who he was about to name as the new state senator."

"How many chances do I get?"

"Only one."

"Then I choose our victim, Judge Farrah Winston."

"Give the man a cigar," said Mort, laughing. "But that's not all. The U.S. Senator from Utah recently announced his retirement, and that seat will be vacated in the election next November."

"So, this must have been what Rosen was talking about. They planned on easing her from the state senate to the U.S. Senate. Okay, so what happened after Judge Winston was murdered? Did the governor appoint someone else?"

"Within a week of her murder," he looked down at the paper he was holding, "George Ogden was appointed. And yes, he voted in favor of the Pilgrim's Cavern project."

Lowell took this in silently for a moment. "What did you find out about Purple Diamond Industries?"

"Nothing. They aren't mentioned anywhere on the web. It's like they don't exist."

Sarah had been sitting at her desk a few feet away pretending not to eavesdrop. Her curiosity finally got the better of her. "So a group of very rich people have decided to build a survival camp complete with room service. What does that have to do with Judge Winston's murder? And how does that help us save poor Johnny?"

"I don't know, yet," said Lowell.

"I have another question," said Sarah. "How could they possibly get rid of the 865 descendants who live in the town?"

"I would guess a lot of brown paper bags exchange hands."

"Hardly seems fair," said Sarah. "So again, what does that mean for us?"

"I'm not sure," said Lowell, "but at least it gives us something to work with. Mort, what do we know about the investors in the project?"

"Absolutely nothing, yet. My guess is it's all been put through a shell company meant to misdirect any curious eyes.

"Get to work on it. Let's see if you can follow the trail back to the rat's nest. We don't have a lot of time, so let's not waste any."

"I'll go change into my hunter outfit."

Chapter Thirty-Two

Andy picked up Lowell, Melinda, and Johnny after a long day in court, a lot of it spent waiting, and drove them uptown to the townhouse. Since it began serving as the temporary address of Starlight Detective Agency, all five floors including the basement were in full use.

Sarah and Mort were in the den watching the evening news when they arrived. Lowell tossed his leather jacket onto a tall wooden coat rack in the hallway.

"You're on TV!" Mort shouted.

Lowell and Melinda were on TV exiting the courtroom.

"Why did your client kill Judge Winston?" The reporter's microphone inches from Melinda's face.

"Was this a vengeance killing? Or was there more to it?"

"Was she the judge's lover?" asked the reporter from Fox.

"No comment," said Melinda repeatedly to the camera, her face filling the screen.

"Would you mind shutting that thing off?" Lowell turned and left the room and headed downstairs to his office.

Melinda gave a look at Sarah and Mort that said *don't ask.* Lowell didn't like being on TV. It never amounted to anything good.

◇◇◇

Lowell was back upstairs in five minutes. The group was sitting around the dinning room table.

"I was just about to call you. Dinner is ready," said Julia, as she served Lowell a plate of organic multigrain pasta with a rich homemade all-organic sauce

Lowell looked down at the scrumptious meal he realized he was never going to get to eat. "Everyone has to leave immediately."

"What's wrong? asked Melinda.

"Someone's been in my office. I can tell. Something is very wrong."

Melinda picked up on what her father was saying immediately. "Oh, my God, there's another bomb, isn't there?"

"Maybe. I don't know for sure. But I don't want to take any chances. I want you all out of here now while I search."

"Where do you think it is?" asked Johnny.

"It could be almost anywhere."

"We have to search this entire building from top to bottom now," said Melinda.

"Don't be stupid. You all have to leave now. I'll search the house alone."

"I suggest we investigate each floor together as a group," replied Melinda ignoring him, "rather than running around haphazardly. That way we can be more thorough and finish quicker."

Johnny interrupted. "There are several logical places it would be. As low in the building as possible, to cause more damage, or where the most people would be, like a living or dining room."

Despite the chill, Lowell ordered everyone out into the backyard. "Melinda, please call the police. I am going to the basement."

Johnny didn't budge.

"I told everyone to leave, and that includes you."

"Easy, big daddy." She had an odd grin on her face. "This is what I do. Get it?"

"I will not have you risk your life to save a building. I can always repair any damage done, but I can't fix you."

"You saved my life by bailing me out of jail. And now you and your daughter are trying to prove me innocent. There's nothing I can ever do to repay you. Let me do this. I'm the best there is at it."

◊◊◊

In the basement, Johnny tilted her head like a cocker spaniel listening to a far-away noise only she could hear. She walked around the room barely making a sound. Then she stopped.

"It's here," she pointed at Lowell's desk "It's under here."

She got on her knees and examined the bomb. "You want the good news or the bad first?"

"Just tell me."

"The good news is it's not a remote control. It's running on a timer, so there's no chance someone can blow it up while we're standing here."

"And the bad news?"

"We got about ten minutes before it goes off."

"What can I do?"

"Get me some tools. I need a wire cutter, a pair of long-nosed pliers, a small screwdriver and a lot of luck."

Lowell bolted up the stairs and returned with a toolbox.

Johnny flipped open the lid, searched around for the right tools, and began to work on the bomb. She removed its casing and unscrewed the connections holding the wires.

"It has a safety on it, a false set of decoy wires. They put those on it to make it difficult to do what I'm doing."

The timer showed one minute.

"Johnny, are you sure? There's still time to get out."

She held up two sets of wires.

"One is the real one, and one is the dummy. If you cut the dummy wires you set off the damn thing instantly."

"So how do you know which is which?"

She took a deep breath, held the two wires in her hand, and said: "You can't."

The timer showed ten seconds. Nobody was leaving the building now.

"Then how do you decide?" a bit of sweat running down his knit shirt.

"The same way I did in the army when I saved a squad from a terrorist's homemade cup of soup like this one."

The clock showed eight seconds.

"And how was that?"

"Eenie meenie minie..."

Chapter Thirty-Three

Lieutenant Roland entered the townhouse with another officer.

"This is officer Loonan. His specialty is explosive devises."

"Where did you find it?" asked Loonan.

"It was under my desk." Lowell walked them to the scene. "We left it where we found it."

Loonan got on his knees and examined the bomb. "Christ. It would have blown you clear through the roof."

"Who found it?" asked Roland.

"Johnny."

Roland raised an eyebrow.

"Maybe she knew where it was," said Roland. "Did she defuse it?"

"Well, you don't think I did, do you?"

"This has a set of dummy wires," said Loonan. "How would she have known which ones to cut?"

"You wouldn't believe me if I told you."

"Well, I think it's rather suspicious," said the officer, as he prepared to take the now impotent bomb out to a waiting police van.

Roland stayed behind for another moment. "You really can't ignore this anymore. You have a crazy woman living with you. I can have her bail revoked tonight, if you like."

"That won't be necessary. I think we have this under control."

The lieutenant laughed. "Under control? She almost blew up the whole block. How do you think your neighbors would feel about that?"

"Hyperbole doesn't suit you, lieutenant."

"Hype what? Oh never mind. How is the case going?"

"Fine."

"That's not what I've been hearing. I think you got nothing. And I think she's panicking and desperate to put the blame on someone else. This would be a good way to do so, don't you think?"

"Not if she was killed along with us."

"But she wasn't, was she? She managed to disarm it just in time. Made herself out to be a big hero in the process. I'll let you know what they come up with after they examine the bomb further."

"Thank you, I would appreciate it."

Roland looked around him. "It would've been a shame if such a beautiful house blew up."

Lowell couldn't tell if it was sarcasm or envy he heard in Roland's voice. A combination of both, he finally decided.

He walked Roland to the front door.

"I'll be extra careful," he said, shaking the Lieutenant's hand. "And thank you for your help."

◇◇◇

"What did he say?" asked Melinda.

"He thinks Johnny's responsible for it all and that it's just a matter of time before she succeeds in killing us. What do you think?"

"I think Lieutenant Roland is a..."

"Yes, I'm sure you do."

Lowell went back downstairs and joined Mort. They ran the recorder back carefully watching the monitor as it showed the backyard. It took until the second playing for Lowell to see it. "Freeze it. Look at that."

Mort stopped the tape, leaned over, and looked at the monitor. "What?"

"Just wait a second. Run it back a bit and watch the lower right-hand corner."

Mort rewound the digital tape a few seconds and played it back. In the bottom of the screen suddenly the tail end of a black squirrel appeared running across the yard by the back door.

"Okay, so a squirrel ran by. I've seen New York's wildlife before. You think he set off the sensor detector? I thought it was programmed to ignore anything under a certain size."

"It is. Just watch."

As they watched, another black squirrel darted across the yard in the exact same place. It was followed a minute later by a third, and a fourth.

"Son of a bitch," said Mort. "They looped it."

"They must not have seen the squirrel. Evidently someone got in here, set the bomb up and then tried to cover their tracks in a hurry."

"But there was someone in the house all day, wasn't there?"

Lowell picked up the house phone. "Julia, would you mind coming downstairs for a minute?"

She walked down the steps.

"Was anyone in my office today?"

"Oh, no, sir. Nobody would come in here without your permission."

"You're sure?"

"Absolutely."

"Were you in the house all day?"

"I was here all day. I didn't even go to the store. I only went out once for a few minutes when there was that big noise. But I never left the front of the house."

Lowell and Mort exchanged a glance.

"What noise?" asked Mort.

"Well, it was a little past noon. Sarah went to Staples and Andy went with her, you know, like you said, nobody should go out alone. But I was still here making corn bread when there was a big explosion across the street. I ran to the front door. I've been a little jumpy lately. When I got outside a man from Con Ed came over and talked to me."

"What about?" asked Lowell.

"He was telling me not to worry. That it was just a boiler accident in a vacant building. He was very friendly. Every time I tried to go back inside he had something else to tell me. Like how to save money on the electric bill, did we ever have our wiring checked, all sorts of things."

"I assume you turned off the alarm while you were outside?"

"Of course. If I left the door open more than a few seconds it would have gone off, so I had to shut it down. But I stayed right by the front door."

"How long were you out there?"

"Couldn't have been more than five minutes or so."

Mort and Lowell exchanged a glance. "Thank you."

"Will you two be coming up for dinner?"

"In a little while."

"Okay, I'll keep it warm." She headed up the stairs.

Mort went back to watching the replay on the screen. "They looped all the cameras on the system through the computer, inside the house and outside. Someone was quite knowledgeable."

"So it's useless?"

"Well, yeah, that system is. But remember a couple of months ago when I talked you into putting in several cameras to cover the stairs? Well, I never got a chance to connect the feeds into the main system, and so they work independently. Whoever was in here couldn't know that. Maybe one of the cameras hidden there caught something."

He went to the stairs and opened a camouflaged panel in the wall. Inside was a tiny digital camera, which he removed. He then plugged it into the computer and pushed *play*. For about two seconds a man's form appeared.

"Run it back. Can we get a better shot of him?" asked Lowell.

"Not with this software."

"Plug it into my main computer and double-click *Delaney* on the desktop, then click on *video*, and then try again."

Mort did as suggested and was able to enhance the picture to near perfection. "Delaney, huh? I've worked with some of his technique. This is as good as I've ever seen."

"He's a genius with this stuff. This uses theoretical input to determine a person's features. It was originally invented for the military, but it's being used by everyone from the police to casinos. Video enhancement is big business, and Delaney continues to improve on it."

"Are you going to bring this to Lieutenant Roland?"

"Not yet. What have I got? A two-second shot of a man on my staircase? That hardly qualifies as proof. I'm afraid I'll have to find more evidence before I could convince him of Johnny's innocence."

Mort froze the picture and they sat staring at the face of their assailant. He was a large, powerfully built blond man, with no discernible humor in his face.

"You know him?"

"Not yet," replied Lowell, staring at the man who had put his home at risk and his loved ones at death's door, "but I will."

Chapter Thirty-Four

Saturday was beautiful, and it had turned unseasonably warm again. It was the end of November but felt more like early autumn. Sunshine stroked the sky as a fall breeze meandered across Manhattan Island. It was eight in the morning. Lowell sat out in the backyard with his coffee and the *New York Times* listening to the birds and their morning gossip. *It must have been a day just like this when Vernon Duke wrote* Autumn in New York, he thought. Lowell cherished his mornings and got up quite early, even on the weekends. It helped organize his mind for the day. He was on his second cup half an hour later when Johnny appeared.

"Good morning."

"Morning," said Johnny, rubbing the sleep from her eyes. "You always get up this early?"

"If you miss the morning you will be chasing it the rest of the day."

She looked terrible. Her eyes were bloodshot and there were pillow lines across her face. "How do you do it?" She tried to push down a cowlick on the back of her head.

"I don't drink too much."

She laughed. "Is there a second choice?"

Julia came out with a tray and put down a plate of eggs and bacon, rye toast, and a cup of coffee in front of her.

"To the hero who saved my house."

Johnny smiled sheepishly. "It was nothing."

"Nonsense. Anything you want, you just ask. Okay?"

"Okay."

"Mr. Lowell, can I make you something?"

"Not now, Julia, thank you. Maybe a little later."

"You know, breakfast is the most important meal of the day. Everyone says that." She stood her ground.

Lowell laughed. "All right, I'll have some toast."

"And some organic eggs."

"Just toast."

"Yes, Mr. Lowell, toast." She headed back inside. "And eggs," she muttered under her breath.

Johnny attacked her breakfast. "What can we do on the weekend?" she asked, in between bites. "Would it be all right to go out for a little walk?"

"No, I'm afraid not."

Johnny pouted. "Jesus, this is like being in jail."

"The food's much better."

Johnny laughed. "That's true."

"Look, I'm getting a little stir-crazy myself. I need to buy my aquatic friends a new home. Would you like to come along?"

"Oh, God, yes. Anything to get out of here for a few hours."

"But you have to follow my instructions to the letter, is that clear?"

"Absolutely."

He looked at his watch. "They open at ten on Saturdays, so after we eat and shower, let's take a ride over there."

At ten-fifteen Johnny was waiting by the front door chatting with Mort. She was showered and looked more refreshed. Lowell came downstairs a few minutes later.

"Turtleneck, jeans, and loafers again. What a surprise." Johnny teased Lowell.

Mort looked at Lowell seriously. "Are you sure going out is such a good idea?"

"We should be all right. The limo has been checked and rechecked, and we'll have Andy with us. Besides, I don't think they'll try anything in broad daylight. That doesn't seem to be their style."

Once outside the front door, Lowell saw the police car parked out front. A little late, but still welcome. Andy was talking to the cop in the car, the limo idling nearby. Johnny and Lowell came down the steps, climbed into the limo, and headed to the Cuddles and Puddles pet store on the ground floor of a classic four-floor walk-up on Second Avenue, sandwiched between a nail salon and a tanning place. Once inside, Johnny was like a kid in a pet store. She went up and down the aisles talking to the birds and tapping on the fish tanks. The puppies got much of her attention, until it was time to pick out the new home that Buster and Keaton would share.

The salesman was quite helpful. Lowell had known him for years. "These two are the top of the line for little fellows like yours," he said. "With each there is a continuous flow of recycled water and enough room for them to grow to their heart's content."

"What do you think," Lowell asked Johnny.

"You want me to decide?"

"Sure."

She looked at both tanks then asked the salesman: "Which is easier to clean?"

"This one has a flushing system that filters the water as it recycles."

"How often do you have to change the filter?"

"Once every three months," said the salesman.

"How about this one?"

"That also has a filtering system, but the filter only has to be washed out, not replaced."

"But which one does a better job?"

"I would say the one with the replaceable filter. It's a bit more work and the filters cost a few bucks, but it cleans the water better."

"Then that's the one I would take."

"Done," said Lowell.

Johnny was over by the parrots as the salesman was ringing up the sale.

"We may not be here much longer," he told Lowell.

"Why?"

"The landlord is tripling the rent. It's too much for my boss to keep the place. It's so stupid. Why would he throw us out after all these years, especially when the economy is in such bad shape?"

Lowell knew the answer to that. "Greed."

Lowell told him to send the equipment the following Friday to the townhouse. He would then retrieve his little friends and move them in with everyone else.

◇◇◇

When they got back to the townhouse Melinda was waiting anxiously. "Can we talk?"

They went downstairs to his office.

"Mort showed me the video."

"Good. I want you to be aware of this man and watch yourself. But under no circumstances are you to approach him or let him know that you recognize him if you cross his path."

"What can we do?"

"I'm not sure yet. But don't worry. I'll take care of it."

"He's," she hesitated, "a very large man. I want you to be careful."

He kissed her on the forehead. "Thank you for worrying, but I'll be fine. I just have to be prepared, that's all."

"Your favorite piece of advice. So what about Johnny? What's going to happen to her once this is all over, even if we do, by some miracle, get her off?"

"She'll go back to her life. Our job is to prove her innocence and then put her back on her path and send her on her way."

"And that's it?"

"How about if she moves in here permanently as my personal bartender?"

"Will you be serious?"

"You are not responsible for every stray cat that crosses your path."

"There's got to be something we can do for her."

"We're trying to save her life."

"You know, speaking of which," said Melinda, "Johnny did save your house, and probably your life."

"I know."

"And she's going to need a hand no matter how this turns out."

"As I told you when you first showed me her chart, this is a complicated person with some difficult manifestations of her neuroses, including alcoholism, a gambling problem and rather loose sexual morals."

"Oh, don't be such a prude," said Melinda. "She also has a strong sense of honor and duty and seems to have earned the respect of her coworkers."

"I'm just letting you know that I am aware that her difficulties extend beyond her current situation."

"And are you planning on doing anything about it?"

Lowell sighed a deep, resonating moan and shook his head. "I suppose you're right. She did save our house."

"Our house?"

"Of course. When I bought it after the divorce I put it in both our names. Your mother gets more than enough from me as it is. I thought you might like to live here someday, you know, when I croak."

"Oh, Dad."

"And it's not money, so you don't have to feel guilty about taking it. If you don't take it, the probate court will, and that would be a shame. I just can't think of anyone who would enjoy it and take care of it the way you would. And I've grown quite attached to my urban castle."

"You know I love this place, too. The neighborhood, the backyard; what's not to love about it?"

"So you'll do it? You'll take over the place when the time comes?"

"Well, all right, but I can't promise that I'll live here the rest of my life."

"Still can't make a commitment, can you? I'll be dead, f'chrisake; it's not like I'm about to call you up and wail, *You promised to live there. What the hell are you doing in Anchorage?* You can do what you want to then. Just agree to it now."

"Anchorage?"

"It would serve you right to go there if you didn't live here."

She laughed. "All right, Dad."

Chapter Thirty-Five

The sidewalk in front of the courthouse was getting busy. It was nearly lunchtime on Monday, and a dozen food carts offering a diverse selection of affordable culinary treats stood in a row on Centre Street waiting for the noon rush. Aromas mixed and mingled together, tempting to the choosiest palette. A few early birds came by and were rewarded with quick service, insuring a relatively leisurely meal. It was still ten minutes before noon, when the crowds would emerge from the buildings and swoop down on these portable restaurants like crows in a field of sweet corn. These vendors made the vast majority of their income each day in that one hour between noon and one. A few rainy weeks could ruin them. Today it was sunny, and they were happy.

A blond man in a long overcoat was leaning against a tree in the park across the street, watching the courthouse. He held a newspaper, occasionally turning the page. But his eyes never left the building. He glanced at his watch and shifted to the other side of the tree.

At noon the courthouse doors opened, and throngs of people exited, the food trucks suddenly surrounded by the hungry.

Johnny and Melinda came out about ten after twelve. They were met by Andy, and the three walked across Centre Street to the park.

Three children were playing tag around a giant tree. Melinda watched them. This was not a residential neighborhood and she absently wondered whose children they were. No parental figure was near by.

"Everything okay?" asked Andy, as they sat on a bench.

"Fine," said Melinda. "It's just some paper work we have to take care of. We'll finish up after lunch. It shouldn't take much longer."

Johnny looked miserable.

"Are you hungry?" asked Melinda.

Johnny sighed. "Not really, but I guess I should eat something."

"What would you like?"

"I don't care much. Any kind of sandwich would do."

Melinda took out some money and handed it to Andy. "Would you mind getting us all something for lunch? Just get a variety."

"Sure. But it might take a few minutes for this crowd to thin out."

He got up and walked over to the row of trucks and stood on the shortest line.

"How do you think it's going?" asked Johnny.

"I think everything is going fine."

Johnny kept rubbing her hands together nervously. She watched the children for a few moments. The little boy had a ball, which he repeatedly offered to the little girl only to pull it back again and again. The girl started crying, and then the boy gave her the ball. She stopped crying and smiled.

"I haven't seen your father all day."

"He had some research to do. But he'll be at the townhouse later."

Johnny smiled. "Good."

Melinda turned away so Johnny couldn't see her joker's grin. "You like my father, don't you?"

"Yes, I do. He's a very smart man, and you've both been so wonderful to me I don't know how I can ever repay you. It's just so unusual to me. Everyone I meet wants something, usually money or sex. But you guys don't seem to be looking for anything. What is it you get out of helping people?"

"Well, it's just the right thing to do, that's all."

"I'm sorry," said Johnny, "I just don't understand."

"I think you do. Why did you risk your life to save your comrades?"

"But that's different. They were people I knew. And it was my job."

"Well, sometimes life puts us in each other's path and we are forced to act how our conscience dictates. Now we know you. And this is our job."

Johnny thought about that for a moment and then nodded.

Andy returned with three sandwiches and sodas.

"I got tuna, chicken salad, and turkey. I'll eat any of them, so you two decide."

"I'd like the tuna, if that's okay," said Johnny.

"Give me the turkey," said Melinda.

They ate their meal in silence for a few moments.

When they'd finished their meal Johnny wanted to walk around a bit, but Andy said no, so they returned to the courthouse.

The blond man watched them leave, and then turned and began walking uptown on Centre Street. After a few blocks he pulled out his cell phone and made a call. "Yeah, it's me. I got them marked, all except that Lowell guy. I can take them out anytime. You just let me know."

He hung up and walked up Lafayette Street through Chinatown, Little Italy and into Soho. At Spring Street he went into the subway and took the 6 train uptown to 42nd Street. He got off, walked down Lexington to 38th Street, and stopped in front of a small building on the side street midway between Lex and Park.

He carried himself with an air of self-assurance, never once looking over his shoulder or he might have noticed that Sarah had followed his every step.

The man took out a key, opened the door, and entered the building.

Shortly thereafter, Lowell, who'd been Sarah's back-up, but too recognizable to take a chance tailing the man directly, picked her up in a cab and they headed uptown.

Chapter Thirty-Six

Mort was bouncing in his chair when Lowell got back to the townhouse office.

"I found out some interesting things about the late Judge Winston."

"Do tell."

"She disappeared for two weeks in August. Nobody knew where she was, not even her watchdog, Larry Rosen. Although she was officially on vacation, it was apparently unlike her to just vanish. There were several inquiries at the time through official but discreet channels, but apparently nobody found out where she had gone."

"And you were able to find all this out how?"

"They weren't *that* discreet."

"Ah, the good old Internet," said Lowell. "The invention that ate humanity."

"She came back in time to return to work, and that's the end of the trail."

"According to Mark Milford, that would be about the time she broke off her previous affair. So what could happen on a romantic vacation that would lead to a total break-up?"

"What if she was becoming too involved with someone, maybe someone with a wife?"

"They did go great lengths to hide their involvement."

"Maybe she was losing control over her emotions," said Mort. "What if she was too much in love and wanted to end an untenable situation? And what if the lover didn't want to end it?"

"That's a lot of what-ifs."

"So just who is this mysterious lover?"

"I don't know." Lowell picked up Judge Winston's chart. "But I think it's about time we found out." He tugged on his ponytail. "Are you getting any feelings about it?"

Mort scrunched up his face. "It was someone in the legal profession, but otherwise I'm not getting much."

"Well, that at least narrows it down a bit."

"What are you going to do?"

"Someone involved in this mess had an affair with the victim that ended suddenly shortly before her murder. I'm going to find out who it was and why it ended."

"Going to do some of your astrology hocus-pocus?"

"Seems the only way."

"What can I do to help?"

"I need the birth information of all of the players in this drama, including the birth time, whenever possible."

"You've got Rosen's and Milford's, who else do you need?"

"If I knew that, it would be easy. I want every man associated with her, and with this case."

"Everyone?"

Lowell nodded. "I want her clerk's clerk, her legal secretary, the other judges, everyone."

"How about if I start with you and me?"

"I think you can probably skip us."

"Just trying to be thorough."

Mort worked on the computer the rest of the day and evening compiling the necessary information. Most of the birthdates of those working at the courthouse including the judges and clerks were easily accessible on the Internet. But some of the information took a bit of hacking.

Once Lowell had a partial list of prospective men he began. It was mostly a matter of grunt work. He had to punch up all of their charts and draw a comparative and a composite with Farrah Winston's. He took each person associated with the case and compared his chart with the victim's. Then he computed the midpoint chart of the two, creating a composite chart, he then computed the Davison relationship chart, and made his notes on each. There were a number of separate charts for each individual, and it took time.

Most of them were superficial in their diagnosis; enough connection to work together or for frivolous socializing, but not for anything more serious. It takes a lot of karma for a meaningful relationship to develop between two souls, and in composite astrology charts that connection would not be easily mistaken.

Mort went to bed about midnight. Lowell worked well into the morning hours, finally falling asleep on the small sofa in his office.

But not before finding what he sought.

Melinda tapped Lowell's shoulder as he lay on the couch. Charts were scattered haphazardly on his chest and on the floor.

"I'm awake. Just my eyes are closed. Look at these, would you?" He handed Melinda the clutch of papers in his hand. "Farrah Winston's lover is one of these."

She looked at them one at a time. "It's not this one. Mars is in the 2nd House conjunct Saturn. Ugg, not a sexual connection." She looked at another. "Not this one either, with Venus and the Sun in the 11th House chart, probably good friends, not lovers."

She picked another one up. "Oh boy, the Sun conjuncts Mars and Jupiter in the 8th House of sex. This would be my guess."

He smiled, eyes still closed.

"I noticed you didn't put any names on these. Who is it?"

He told her.

"Oh, my God."

◇◇◇

Lowell took a quick shower, tugged a brown turtleneck over his head and pulled on matching socks and neatly pressed jeans.

Melinda was sitting on the couch in the basement office, staring at the charts. She looked up at Lowell as he came down the stairs cradling a cup and saucer.

"What are you going to do with this information?"

"Confront him."

"Well, we could…"

"Without you," he interrupted.

Before Melinda could respond Mort came in holding several papers in one hand and a cup of coffee in the other. "I traced that address you gave me for the hitman. The building is managed by a small real estate firm. They rented it to a company called World Wide Markets, which doesn't seem to have a permanent address, just a P.O. box. I was able to trace the check they used to pay for the box."

"Let me guess—it's a phony."

"Yep. The bank account was closed the next week."

He pulled out another piece of paper. "They sent their paperwork though a shell company with only a mail drop. There isn't much of a trail but I'm used to that. Everyone leaves breadcrumbs behind if you know where to look. I'll find them."

"At least we now know what P.C. stands for," said Lowell, "whatever good that does us."

"What a tangled web," said Melinda.

"But if you gently pull the threads, it all untangles."

"Well, you'd better pull them quickly," said his daughter, "or it will be a moot point if Johnny is convicted."

Chapter Thirty-Seven

Judge Thompson sat behind his massive desk. Lowell sat facing him.

"Mr. Lowell, I have a very few minutes to spare. What can I do for you?"

"It involves the Winston murder case, your honor. Some new evidence has come to light that I think you should be aware of."

"This is a matter for the DA's office. Why are you bothering me with it?"

"I think you'll understand by the time I am finished."

"All right, get on with it."

"Before I begin, I wish to explain a little of what I do, as many people have a preconceived notion about astrology. I practice both personal astrology and what is called mundane, or world event astrology. I am also an astro-economist."

"A what?"

"Over the past twenty years I have been employed by various banks, hedge funds, and other financial institutions as a market analyst. Because I and other traders use astrology as one of our main tools in commodities trading we have coined the term *astro-economist*. It has been used a number of times in *Barron's*, the *Wall Street Journal*, and other financial publications where I am periodically interviewed or quoted. My list of personal clients has included well known artists, financiers, and government officials."

"What has any of this to do with this case?"

"I feel it necessary to list some of what I have been able to accomplish using astrology as a precursor to my main point."

The judge waved his hand in a dismissive manner. "Just make it brief, Mr. Lowell. I'm a very busy man."

"Quite briefly then: I predicted the rise of oil to well over a hundred dollars a barrel when it was trading at $32 a barrel years in advance, the collapse of the mortgage business and the housing market, the decay of the banking industry, and the onset of the recession and subsequent market crash. I only mention these events in case you are a non-believer in the celestial arts."

"All right, I am duly impressed. And again I ask what has this to do with this case?"

"I have charted the horoscopes for most of the people involved in this case and cross-referenced them via what we call composite and comparative charts. These charts show the potential a relationship has. It can not predict if the two will ever meet, but it can determine the type of relationship that would occur if they did. I believe I can show that there were others with a much stronger motive to kill Farrah Winston than the defendant's."

The judge was silent.

"There were several people whose charts demand we further investigate their connection to the victim. One was a lover she had taken about eighteen months ago."

"And you plan on introducing this as evidence in my courtroom?"

"Yes, your honor."

"Over my dead body. What do you think you're doing?"

"Trying to save an innocent woman's life."

"By dragging other innocent people into the spotlight? I don't think you realize just what your prodding may produce."

"I think I do. And if anyone knows what trouble it may cause it is you, your honor."

"I don't like your implications, sir." His voice was booming, but it had lost its authority, and they both knew it.

"Let me tell you what I do know. You and Judge Winston were having an affair. It lasted about eighteen months, and it looks like you did a very good job of keeping it secret."

Thompson stood up and began to pace for a few moments and then sat in his towering judge's chair. To Lowell he suddenly seemed like a little boy who had climbed into his father's forbidden seat and got caught.

"Again I resent your tone of voice." The judge's voice was much softer. "It was no torrid affair, nor was it something I planned. It just happened. We met at a charity fundraiser and, and it just sort of…" he trailed off. "How did you know?"

"It was quite obvious to me. Your comparative and composite charts both spoke of a strong sexual attraction. And there were transits over the past eighteen months that could easily have led to a liaison. And since you two had many opportunities to meet I assumed the rest."

The judge got up from his chair and went to the window. "When I first heard you were on the witness list I was afraid it might come to this. You know, I've always believed in astrology. As a child my mother would take me and my brother to Coney Island to visit a gypsy woman. Every birthday she would draw up our charts and forecast our fortunes for the coming year. And you know what? She was always right, always right. When I got older and my mother finally died at ninety-one, I went to my childhood home and had to throw out all that stuff."

He was looking out the window as he spoke.

"I found some of the notes she had written about us through the years and what she saw for the long-term, and as I read them the hairs on my arms went straight up. Almost everything she had predicted for me and my family had come true. When I was a little boy she even predicted that I would have a career in the legal profession and could very well become a judge."

He stood there in silence for a few moments, and then shook his head suddenly. He turned to Lowell. "You don't think I killed her, do you?"

"I don't know. The charts do not show a violent nature to your relationship. But as I have learned, anyone is capable of murder. They do however show a distancing between you shortly before she died."

"It's true. We had broken off our relationship about a month before her murder."

"Why was that?"

"Many reasons. I think Farrah needed something from me, and once she got what she needed the relationship became superfluous."

"What was it that she got?"

"The differences between us made her question things she had never really looked at with an open mind."

"There was quite an age difference."

"That was the least of our differences, and the most superficial. She was raised in a Republican family that could trace its roots to the Mayflower. I was, and am, a liberal Democrat and I will go to my grave fighting the decay and class separation that are destroying our society."

"You had disagreements with her?"

"At first all we did was argue. But it was a respectful, seductive kind of skirmish. Even after we started sleeping together we would have enthusiastic battles of political ideology. After a while she stopped fighting and starting listening. All her life she had been surrounded by people with the same political perspective; isolated in childhood, attending conservative schools and meeting mostly young Republicans. Even in a liberal New York law school, she managed to surround herself with other like-minded people and only saw things from her rather limited point of view. But by the time we met, the world had changed. Her eyes were already being opened to the plight of the poor and middle class, and she began to see what was happening in this country. That's when she started to change."

"Why did you finally break up?"

"It was becoming more dangerous for us to meet. If my wife found out, it would be disastrous. It was just a matter of when we'd be discovered."

He stood and walked to the window and looked out.

"Mr. Lowell, I love my wife. She is a bright, vivacious woman, beautiful in every way. Not a day goes by that I'm not thankful she's in my life. When I met Farrah, well, I was just awestruck, I guess. You've seen pictures of her, but they don't begin to show the depth and charms she possessed. She was beautiful, but so much more. The kind of woman men dream about. I never expected anything to come of it. Then slowly, after running into each other a few times, we made a date. It was only supposed to be coffee. But it turned into much more. How could I refuse her gift? Would you?"

He sat back down and poured a glass of water. He took a sip and continued. "If this were to come out, it would ruin my life. What good would it do to destroy my marriage and career?"

"Why didn't you excuse yourself from the case?"

"I tried. But they wouldn't let me. How could I quit without telling them about my affair?"

"Aren't you concerned someone might have seen you together and recognized you from your vacation to the Caribbean?"

"You knew about that, too?"

"Yes."

The judge nodded.

"You're right. We worked so hard to conceal it. I don't want my face showing up on the Internet. I'm afraid someone will identify me if they see my picture next to hers. I plan to ban all computers and cameras from the courtroom and hope for the best."

"I am only interested in saving that poor girl's life," said Lowell. "I am convinced that she didn't do it and that someone who works in this courthouse set her up. I have no interest in dragging you into this, if possible."

The judge looked relieved.

"But if Joanna Colbert is convicted, we will be forced to bring it all out into the open and demand a retrial."

"I'm afraid you can't count on my help with this. Any unusual activity in this case will be scrutinized thoroughly. I can't even grant you a continuance." Judge Thompson put his head in his hands. "Why did this case have to fall into my lap?"

"Do you know anyone who might have wanted to kill her?"

Thompson shook his head. "Everyone who knew her loved her. Even if you didn't agree with her opinion, she was such a caring person that people of all political persuasions enjoyed her company. I can't imagine why someone would want her dead. Frankly, I was hoping it was your client." He sat back in his chair and closed his eyes. "So now what?"

"The only way I can save Johnny Colbert's life is to discover who did kill Farrah Winston."

"I'm afraid uncovering the truth won't be enough. You've got to prove it, too. There are some powerful people who want to see this case go away quickly, and they will do whatever they can to get a fast conviction. Are you sure your client isn't guilty?"

"I am positive. What do you know about Judge Winston's clerk, Larry Rosen?"

"That little snot nose was always getting under my skin. He would follow her like a deranged suitor and almost caught us on several occasions. He's a little creepy if you ask me. If you want to find someone who had disagreements with her, talk to him."

"I have, and he gave me the impression that he and Judge Winston saw eye to eye on everything."

The judge nodded. "That's just like him to tell you half the story."

"They weren't close?"

"Oh, they were, at first. For a few years she considered Rosen her trusted confidant. But after we became lovers, her relationship with him rapidly deteriorated as she saw what a closed-minded little twerp he really is."

Lowell frowned for a moment. "I'm going to do what I can to keep your name out of this if I can, for now. But in my investigation I might step on a few legal toes and may need your help."

"I'm listening."

Chapter Thirty-Eight

Larry Rosen closed up his desk and turned out the light. It was 5:30 and he was done for the day. He had about a month to clean up Judge Winston's business and put her professional affairs in order. Then he would be assigned to another judge.

He walked out of the courthouse and was about to head toward the subway when a long black stretch limousine pulled up next to him. The back window went down and David Lowell's face appeared.

"Mr. Rosen."

Rosen was startled for a moment. "Mr. Lowell?"

"Please, won't you join me for a few moments? I'd like to talk to you. My driver will take you wherever you wish to go when we're through."

Rosen scratched his chin. "Can't this wait until tomorrow?"

"I'm afraid not. If you just come in I'll explain it all to you. It shouldn't take more than a few minutes."

Rosen looked into the limo. It was quite luxuriously furnished, with comfortable seats. There was even a desk with a computer on top. Well, it beat sitting on the F train.

"Well, all right, but only if we can talk while you drive me to Brooklyn. I have an appointment this evening that I can not be late for, and I must get home in time to prepare."

"Of course."

He got in.

When he was seated, Lowell handed Rosen the phone and pushed a button. "Tell my driver where you would like to be dropped."

Andy came on. "Yes, sir, where would you like to go?"

"Take the Brooklyn Bridge and go up Smith Street," said Rosen. "Make a right on Thirty-seventh and then the first left. It's the third house on the right."

"Very good, sir."

The limo started to move. Lowell opened a cabinet to reveal about two dozen bottles.

"Would you like something? I've got pretty much everything, vodka, scotch, wine, beer. I'm having a vodka and tonic."

"That sound fine, I'll have the same."

"Stoli okay?"

"Sure."

Lowell took two highball glasses, added ice and mixed the vodka and tonic.

"Would you like a slice of fresh lime?

"Yes, lime would be nice."

Lowell took a lime slice from the small refrigerator, stuck it on the side of the glass and handed it to Rosen.

"Here you go." He kept the other drink for himself.

"No lime for you?"

Lowell shook his head and put his hand to his stomach. "Citrus doesn't agree with me."

Rosen squeezed the lime slice into the drink and raised the cup. "To your health," he said, and then took a large gulp.

"No, to yours." Lowell took a long sip. "Ah, quite refreshing."

"So what is so important that you had to tell me now?"

Lowell looked at his watch. "Oh, you'll know in about fifteen seconds."

"What happens in fifteen seconds?"

"You pass out."

"What the hell are you talking ab…" Rosen keeled over and Lowell caught the glass before it hit the floor.

Lowell picked up the phone. "He's out cold."

Andy lowered the glass partition. "Brilliant idea, putting the drug in the lime slice. How long does this stuff last?"

"Not long, maybe ten minutes."

"Well, we'd better hurry."

"You be ready," said Lowell.

"Just give me the signal."

Lowell tied Rosen's hands behind him and put a blindfold over his face as Andy closed the glass divider. Then he turned on Delaney's invention and set the machine to a dark and rainy night on a rural road. Soon the windows were wet and chilly, and "a heavy rain" poured down on the limo. Then Lowell took Rosen's watch and moved it ahead five hours.

He put the drinks out of sight, took a gun from his desk drawer and waited.

A few minutes later Rosen started to groan. "Where am I?"

"You're still in my limousine, and I'm going to ask you a few questions, which you'd better answer truthfully."

"What the hell is this?" He tried to move his hands, but couldn't. "I'm not answering anything, you crazy bastard. I'm going to have you arrested for kidnapping and assault."

"If I were you, I'd answer."

Rosen continued to struggle with his restrains. "The hell I will. What are you going to do if I don't? What's to prevent me from kicking out your window and yelling for help?"

Lowell took the blindfold off.

"God damn you, I'll have you all arrested. You're…" He looked out the window and stopped. Then he noticed the rain pelting the roof. "Where are we?" he asked, a tinge of fear in his voice.

"Western Massachusetts."

"What? How long have I been out?"

Lowell looked at his watch. "Five hours."

Rosen looked out the window. "Why are we in Massachusetts?"

"Because, nobody will ever find your body here. If you don't tell me the truth, and soon, I'm going to kill you and dump you in a lake."

Rosen wasn't a brave man, as Lowell knew from his natal chart. He lacked backbone and had no illusions about it. To save his ass he would sell out his own mother in a heartbeat.

Rosen stared at him. "You couldn't. You wouldn't."

"Oh, but I could and would. You see, Mr. Rosen, I'm trying to save the life of an innocent young woman. And it is obvious to me that the people responsible for the death of Farrah Winston are using my client as a scapegoat. Since they have no compunctions about hurting an innocent bystander, I am forced to act in the most callous of manners."

He put the gun up to Rosen's cheek and pressed it into the flesh.

Rosen was sweating profusely. His breath was short and erratic. He had rarely seen a gun, let alone had one put against his face like that.

"But then you'll never let me go. I could identify you to the police and…" He shut up.

Lowell lowered the gun. "Mr. Rosen, I think by the end of our conversation, going to the police will be the last thing on your mind. I seriously doubt you will tell many people about this meeting."

Rosen shivered. "Would you mind untying my hands? It's most uncomfortable."

Lowell put the gun back up against Rosen's cheek. "If I untie you and you do anything stupid I will have no problem using this. Is that clear?"

Rosen nodded.

Lowell reached behind Rosen and released the restraints, the gun never leaving his hand. Rosen rubbed his wrists and looked at his watch.

"God damn it, I *have* been out for five hours!" He rubbed his neck.

"I want to know why you set up Johnny Colbert to take the fall."

"Because I had to."

"You're not in a position to put this all in motion yourself. Who told you to do this? Was it for money?"

"Money." He laughed. "Money is crap. This was about right and wrong. You have no idea who you're dealing with."

"That, sir, is why your life is still hanging by a thread. Who *am* I dealing with?"

"People that understand. People that want to save this country and get us back on track."

"What about the assassin?"

"Who?"

"Don't play dumb. He was the one who set off the bomb that killed Judge Winston, wasn't he? Or did you do that?"

"I didn't kill anyone. I was just supposed to call a number when the right person came into the courtroom, that's all, nothing else."

"But Farrah Winston is dead because of you, you know that don't you? And an innocent person is on trial for her life. My daughter is going to call you to the stand. If you're willing to testify to what you just told me, I can guarantee your safety."

Rosen laughed a humorless guffaw. "You can't guarantee your own safety. They already tried to kill you, and they'll keep trying until they get you, you know. And if I get anywhere near a courtroom..." He shook his head. "I'm not testifying to anything."

"But if you don't agree to help me, you're dead in about five minutes."

He opened a drawer and took out a silencer, which he slowly screwed on to the gun barrel. "This is your last chance."

Rosen's mouth went dry. "All I know is that they're very powerful men who can get things done."

Lowell continued to screw the silencer on. "Give me a name."

"I don't have one, I swear to you," he shouted. "Please, for God's sake, I don't know anything. I never even met them, only spoken on the phone. I just told them when that foul-mouthed woman started threatening Farrah. I don't know anything else."

"What do you know about Pilgrim's Cavern?"

"I never heard of it. Look, I don't know what you're talking about. I had to help them. Farrah Winston was going to ruin the country."

"How was she going to do that?"

"By becoming the president of the United States someday and pretending to be conservative only to change her agenda once she was in office."

It was starting to make some sort of sense in a bizarre way. "How did these men contact you?"

"Someone phoned me at my office a few months ago. He said that they shared my views on the world and felt that what was happening to America was disgusting. They wanted to take back the power and straighten things out. All they asked was for me to keep my eyes open and let them know if Farrah began acting strangely."

"But why?" said Lowell, pressing the gun harder against his head.

"Because she *was* changing." His voice cracked.

"How?"

"I don't know. It was subtle at first, just little things most people who didn't know her well would miss. The way she talked, how she responded to newspaper editorials, things like that. She was becoming concerned with issues that had never bothered her before."

"And that just wasn't acceptable, is that it? Was she beginning to lean just a tad toward the center? Or even a bit to the left? So what? Surely she was still a conservative in most things. Nobody changes overnight."

"You just don't get it, do you? She was going to ruin everything."

"So you wanted her dead?"

"I didn't want her to die. I didn't know they planned on killing her, or I never would have gone along with it. I swear. They just told me to let them know if there was any trouble in her court, beyond the usual arguments and shouting. When that Colbert girl came in and made such a ruckus, then threatened to kill Farrah, I called the number they gave me and told someone what happened."

"That's all you did?"

"I swear to it." The sweat was running freely down his cheeks, the fear in his eyes excruciatingly present.

"You know something, Rosen—I believe you."

As the wilderness sped by, Lowell turned for a moment to get something from behind him. The road appeared to bend, and the car slowed down. Rosen saw this as his chance. He leaped forward, grabbed the handle of the door and jumped out of the limousine. He expected to be thrown onto the side of the road late at night in a New England forest.

Instead, he was sitting on the sidewalk right in front of his brownstone in the early evening. The limo sped away, leaving Rosen on the concrete, his mouth open in a most unnatural manner.

◇◇◇

After Rosen jumped from the limo Andy headed back to Manhattan. He lowered the partition behind him. "How did it go?"

"It was close," replied Lowell, as he gave Andy his gun back. "For a minute there I didn't think he was going to take the bait and jump. Thank God he did. It would have been very embarrassing to have gone through all of that and then have to open the door and escort him out."

Andy chuckled. "You've got quite a flair for the dramatic, don't you?"

"One of the many questionable traits I inherited from my family."

"Where to, boss?"

"It's almost dinnertime. Let's go home."

Julia was setting the table when they arrived. Lowell went into the den where Melinda was working at her makeshift desk.

"Hi," she said. "How did it go?"

He told her about the limo ride with Rosen. He took out a digital tape of the conversation with Rosen and put it into a portable player.

"It doesn't tell us much," she said. "Besides, it's hearsay without corroboration from Rosen. He could say it was recorded under duress, or altered. We've got to get him on the witness stand."

"That's what I figured."

"Well, I'll add him to the witness list tomorrow. I hope I can get him to incriminate himself. Or at least create reasonable doubt."

"I have no doubt, reasonable or otherwise, that you can do it."

She smiled. "At least we finally have a lead. It's something to work with."

"Yes," said Lowell. "There may be some light at the end of this tunnel after all."

Chapter Thirty-Nine

Early the next day Sarah was in the basement of the townhouse when the phone rang. "Starlight Detective Agency, how may I help you?"

"Sarah, it's Melinda."

"Oh, hi. He's not here right now, but I expect he'll call soon. Any message?"

"Yes. Tell him that Larry Rosen is dead."

Sarah got a chill. "Rosen, isn't he the victim's clerk?"

"That's right."

"What happened?"

"He was run over by a car outside of his brownstone."

"Accident?"

"I somehow doubt it. Tell my father to get in touch with me when you hear from him. He isn't answering his cell phone."

Melinda hung up.

"Jesus," said Sarah to herself, "this thing just gets weirder."

She went upstairs to the kitchen where Julia was preparing dinner. "Could I get a cup of tea?" She didn't really want the tea. She just didn't feel like being alone at the moment.

"Of course," said Julia. "Let me make it for you. What kind do you want?" She held out a tea box with a dozen varieties.

Sarah picked a bag of Constant Comment and put it on the counter. "This one. It's got a nice orange flavor I like."

The phone rang in the office.

"I'd better get that." She ran down the flight of stairs and grabbed it on the fourth ring. "Starlight Detective Agency, how may I help you?"

"I'm in the limo. Any calls?"

"Yes, Melinda just called and said you should get back to her quickly."

"Yes, good. I need to talk to her about preparing for Larry Rosen's testimony."

"You're not going to be able to do that, boss."

"And why not?"

"Rosen's dead. Got run over outside his house this morning."

Silence on the line.

Lowell looked at his watch. Melinda would be in her office. He picked up the phone.

"You heard about Rosen," she said.

"Sarah told me."

"Why did they kill him?"

"Apparently I pulled that thread a little too hard."

"You mean that it was because of us?"

"No," replied Lowell emphatically, "it was because of him and the choices he made. He was at least partially responsible for a murder and an innocent young woman facing life imprisonment. He had to face his karma, cruel an ending as it was."

"What are we going to do now?"

"I don't know."

"Now we really can't use anything Rosen told you in the limo. Without him here to confirm what he said I'm afraid it's useless. There is no proof that was even Rosen speaking, and getting a voice print from him now to compare it to would be rather difficult."

"Would a video tape have been better?"

"In hindsight, yes, but you still would have had to get him to say something more incriminating. Nothing he said would be sufficient to clear our client. So far the prosecutor has Johnny as the only member of an army troop capable of stealing the explosives, building a bomb, blowing up Judge Winston and going home to her little walk-up in the Village. Her neighbors hate her, she can't make a living, and her father used to beat the crap out of her. And there's nothing I can do to help her. Whoever thought this thing out did a hell of a job. I can't figure it out."

"I know what I have to do," said her father. "I'll call you later."

Chapter Forty

Andy drove Lowell to The Starlight Detective Agency's office. With everyone temporarily centered at the townhouse it was eerily silent. As David entered the front door, he froze. Someone had been there, too.

He entered his private office and turned on the overhead light. His swivel chair, which he always left facing the desk, was turned a fraction to the right. A folder on top of one of his many stacks was slightly askew.

He walked to the far wall and took a Monet print down, a small hole in the center of a flower. He took a small penknife and edged it in behind the wood paneling. The piece of plywood came off easily to reveal a small chamber. Inside was the security camera for the office.

He removed the camera, flipped open the little screen and watched as the blond man rummaged through the office, opening drawers, searching the file cabinets. When he had finished his search, he attempted to put things back the way they had been and then left. The expression on his face showed that whatever he was looking for he obviously didn't find. Maybe it was the hard drive.

Lowell knew what he had to do. There was no other way. Their very lives depended on his actions. If he didn't deal with this now, he and his loved ones would never feel safe. But he had to time it exactly right. He began every day reviewing his chart, and he knew that Mars would be on his ascendant late that afternoon and he would need the extra jolt of energy the God of war would give him.

He sat at his desk and pulled out the large bottom drawer. He took a pair of latex gloves and put them on. Next he pulled out a shoulder bag and started filling it with a few odds and ends: a thick number-two pencil, two pool balls, and a tiny digital camera with a wide-angle lens. He picked up a container of baby powder, which he emptied into a zip-lock sandwich bag and then sealed it shut. He took out the revolver he had procured several days before from his incompetent mugger. He cocked the gun, loading one bullet into the chamber, and then replaced the gun clip with one from the drawer. He dropped the gun into the bag, removed the gloves, and headed for the door, hooking an umbrella over his arm.

Lowell exited the building, turned left and started walking west on Twenty-fourth Street. What he needed to do couldn't be done in a limo; it required that he be followed. He sent Andy home and began to walk. He crossed Park Avenue, then Madison and Fifth. The people hustled by, all caught up in their own dramas. The lunch rush was over, and the streets, though active, weren't crowded. It would be easy for the blond man to follow him.

At Seventh Avenue he turned left, walked south three blocks and then turned right onto Twenty-first. Lowell had entered an area of Manhattan that once held countless warehouses. It was still a bit of a commercial zone, though nowhere near what it had once been. This neighborhood also used to be one of the music centers of New York, but the overinflated real estate market of the past decade and subsequent rising rents had put many of the rehearsal and recording studios out of business. There were still a few remaining, as evidenced by a pair of guys walking by carrying guitar casese. But this part of the city was now more of a center for the fashion industry, with a lot of photography studios. Models now far outnumbered guitarists.

He made an act of turning around to see if he was being followed, but he knew, hoped, that he was. The mouse was leading the cat.

◇◇◇

Lowell pushed open an unlocked, papered-over glass door of what was once a thriving bakery. He had come here often in his early years for a cheap espresso and warm croissant. Earlier in the year he had bought the building in hopes of bringing the store back someday, restoring it exactly as he remembered it, down to the rutted plank floors. Lowell felt passionately that these places full of unique tastes and smells had to be as much a part of the new New York as the sterile new cupcake and frozen yogurt outlets. He only awaited a good contractor who would get the job done in his lifetime, though his hair would only get grayer waiting for that miracle to happen.

But he couldn't dwell on that now.

He walked to the back of store, the old counter on his right, opened a half-rotten wooden door, and went down a flight of equally rotten wood stairs.

The blond man approached the outside door, opened it slowly and listened intently. He could hear Lowell walking down the stairs. He walked slowly down the hallway and saw the glow of a light come from the cellar.

When he reached the bottom of the stairs, the blond man saw Lowell casually leaning against a table.

"You have violated my home, threatened my family and friends, and almost blown up my house," said Lowell. "I'd like to know why."

The man looked around him to judge his situation. There were mostly empty shelves along the wall, random items here and there: an old umbrella, some board games, a few books. A large metal mixing machine covered with cobwebs stood alongside the stairs. No other doors. He towered over Lowell by half a foot and licked his lips like a stray dog before a wounded woodchuck.

"It was a job," he finally answered.

"A job? Who hired you?"

"That's none of your business. But it's a job I plan to complete."

The big man moved in and reached toward Lowell, grabbing his coat. Lowell moved one step to his left and took one of the man's enormous hand in his, twisting in an awkward way as his other hand pushed against the big man's elbow. The man went down.

The big man didn't stay down for long. He stood, flexing his arm and grimacing. He moved toward Lowell and put his hands around his throat. Lowell quickly moved back one step and turned the man's hands inward as he swept his foot under the other man's, causing him to stumble.

"What is that? Judo or some sort of crap? You think that nonsense is going to stop me?"

He leaped toward Lowell, grabbing him by the torso, lifting him off the ground and slamming his back against the wall. Lowell groaned, but he reached over to the shelf, grabbed the two pool balls, and smashed them against the man's ears. He let go of Lowell, raising his hands to his head.

Lowell put his left foot against the man and pushed. The man fell against the shelf, tearing it from the wall and opening a gash on his face. He wiped the blood away from his eye and grunted like a wild animal.

He rushed forward, but Lowell had taken a baggie from his pocket and now he threw the baby powder into the man's face. He gagged and was temporarily blinded. Lowell took the brass pipe and with all his might struck the man's shoulder. He howled in pain.

Still the man did not go down.

He wiped the powder from his eyes, reached up with his right hand and grabbed Lowell by the throat again. He squeezed tight. With a gasp, Lowell reached into his coat pocket and took out the revolver. He aimed as carefully as he could and pulled the trigger. The bullet went through the man's left shoulder. The assassin finally released Lowell from his grip.

Lowell stepped back two paces and began to catch his breath. But still the assassin came, an arm hanging uselessly at his side. Lowell raised the gun, but the man grabbed it before he could shoot. He pointed it at Lowell's midsection and fired. Lowell put his hands to his stomach and dropped to his knees in agony.

The hitman stood with the gun still pointed at Lowell.

"Little man, it takes a long time to die from a gunshot to the stomach. I'm going to rip you to pieces a little bit at a time. I'm going to reach inside you and tear your organs out one by one until you beg me to kill you." He wiped the dripping blood from his face. "When I'm done with you I'm going to your townhouse and visit your daughter and that other little girl. I'm going to rip them apart. And then I'm going to enjoy watching the life pour out of them as they struggle for their last breath."

Lowell struggled to speak. "You killed the judge… didn't you?"

"Sure I did. And that little prick Rosen. And now I'm going to kill you."

"How did you… set up… the girl?"

"Rosen kept an eye out for the perfect patsy. When she showed up in court he knew he had what we needed. So I stole some explosives from her army unit and set it all up. It was easy, until you showed up."

"Why?"

"Why what?"

"Why did you kill them?"

"It was a job. This is what I do."

Lowell, on his knees, slumped against a wooden crate and let out a deep groan. "Who…who hired you?"

"I don't know. I never know. They pay me and give me my assignment. What the hell do you care, anyway? You'll be dead soon."

The man turned toward the sound of an ambulance siren outside. When he turned back, the point of an umbrella was headed toward his groin.

The man doubled over, but managed to raise the gun again. "You bastard."

He fired. Lowell didn't flinch. He fired again. Nothing happened. And then Lowell clocked him over the head with the heavy wooden handle of the umbrella, an old piece perfectly decorated with a thick piece of silver at the bend.

The man went down in a heap.

Lowell had the confession he needed on the videocam that he had placed on the shelf when he first arrived. He grabbed the tiny camera, stuffed it into his pocket, and headed for the stairs.

Halfway up, he heard a grunt and felt a hand grab his ankle. The ancient stairs moaned their displeasure at the weight of two men. Lowell grabbed a small metal handrail near the top of the steps and pulled his foot free, but the man was already moving up the stairs.

He had the gun turned around in his hand, ready to crash it down on whatever part of Lowell's body he could reach first when his foot broke through one of the wood steps.

He fell awkwardly sidewise, and his hip hit the stair's runners, torqueing his body up and over, sending him headfirst into the high metal arm of the bakery's old mixing machine and then to the basement floor.

The man's head lay at an unnatural angle, his body drooping against the shelves.

Lowell slumped onto the floor of the bakery and leaned against the end of the counter. The skin of his neck throbbed and his back would hurt for weeks, but nothing was broken. He was sure more places would ache as the shock wore off.

What hurt the most right now was the sting of where the blank had hit his abdomen. Lowell knew, today, that he had overestimated his physical talents, but he still had a few good tricks, including those latent acting skills.

Lowell had gambled on that, and won, if the death of an adversary, no matter how loathsome, could be called winning. After all, the man dead downstairs was just one of the real killers of Judge Winston and Larry Rosen, and the only consolation today came from clearing Johnny's name. His work was far from over.

Lowell stood up, brushed off his clothes, and tried to retie his pony tail. He gave up, stretched his back, and took out his cell phone. Ten minutes later Andy arrived, followed closely behind by two squad cars.

Chapter Forty-One

That evening, Lowell rested in front of a roaring fire. He didn't believe in prescription painkillers, but a little Advil and a cold beer couldn't hurt. And it didn't.

Melinda sat by his side and reached out to give him a hug.

"Easy does it. I'm still quite sore."

"Sorry, but I'm just so happy to know that Johnny didn't… well you know."

"Yes, I'm happy, too."

He had quietly told her about the day's events, not wanting to get Johnny's hopes up just yet. Nothing was final until the judge dismissed the case.

Lowell took a long draw from the beer glass. "Roland wants to discuss the video first thing tomorrow, and we'll go from there."

"Father, I can't thank you enough. For what you did. For Johnny. For me." She patted her father's hand very gingerly. "And for this fire. It always means home and comfort to me."

The next morning, Lowell Advilled-up again and went to the precinct house. Roland was waiting for him.

"Well, that was quite a performance, Lowell. Oscar material. I never thought of you as the physical type. Obviously I was wrong."

"I've told you repeatedly about my black belt in aikido."

"I never gave much credibility to it until now."

"I guess you were wrong about Johnny Colbert."

"I guess so."

He held up a folder. "The lab did a rush job on the gun we found by his body."

"Thank you. You do know that he was just the muscle. We need to follow the path back to the brains behind all of it."

"His prints aren't in any of our files. We'll send them and his picture to the F.B.I. and Interpol. The only lead we've got is from you about the townhouse where he was staying. I'll follow up on it." His voice lacked conviction.

"You'll discover that it was rented to a shell company with a P.O. box taken out under a fictitious name. The rental deal was done over the phone. The tax ID number for the credit check was a scam. The company was put together right before, and the bank account that the check was drawn on was closed the next week. The lease was sent to the P.O. box and returned by mail."

"I see you've been busy."

"But surely if you follow the trail you should be able to find its origin."

Roland shook his head. "We haven't got the resources to chase this thing."

Lowell frowned. "That's not like you to give up so easily. What's going on?"

"Look, we've got Farrah Winston's murderer, that's what we set out to do. And you've exonerated your client, isn't that enough?"

"I'm afraid not. I have been targeted for murder and I can not let that go, nor will I live in constant fear that someone someday will decide I am a liability they can not afford."

"All I can tell you is that officially this case is closed. I've been told to let sleeping dogs lie, in those exact words."

"Someone tried to stonewall my investigation, and now you're getting pressure to drop the case. Doesn't that bother you?"

"Of course it does, but what would you like me to do? My hands are tied."

"Well, mine aren't."

"I would be careful not to step on the wrong toes, if I were you."

"Thank you for your concern."

"Look, I don't know how much I can help you, but if there's anything within my means let me know."

◇◇◇

Lowell met Judge Thompson in his chambers. He brought a laptop computer and a copy of the video with him.

"You don't look so good," said the judge.

A bruise on Lowell's face had deepened into a rich eggplant purple. Lowell wasn't sure when in the struggle he got banged there.

"Sometimes the path to the truth is not an easy journey."

"What did you want to show me?"

"I believe this evidence will exonerate my client."

He opened the laptop and inserted the disc. For twenty minutes Judge Thompson sat spellbound and watched as Lowell and the hit man went at it. When Lowell was seemingly shot in the stomach the judge grunted loudly in sympathy. When it was over he sat back in his chair, his finger supporting his chin.

Finally he looked over at Lowell. "I take it you weren't really shot. And how old are you?"

"Over fifty."

The judge closed his eyes for a moment. "That was quite something for a man of any age."

"I almost didn't make it. I was prideful of my skills."

"But you made it. And this man was responsible for both murders."

"He was the puppet, but I still don't know who was pulling the strings."

"I assume this can all be corroborated?"

"Lieutenant Roland has seen this video and is now in possession of the body and other physical evidence. He said he will call you later."

"Well, let me speak to him and put all of this in order. I want a meeting with all the principals tomorrow. My clerk will set it up with the district attorney's office and be in touch with you."

"Your honor, one other thing. Were you aware of the plans to project Farrah Winston into national politics?"

Thompson shot forward in his chair. "How on earth do you know about that?"

"I had a reliable source."

"Very few people knew this. She had been approached by a group of ultraconservative businessmen with old money. They wanted to push her onto the national scene and bankroll her future with a fortune."

"And with the sudden death of Senator Smith, she was going to be appointed state senator in Utah."

"They were all set to make the announcement."

"And then what?"

"There was an opening next November for the U.S. Senate seat, and she was being groomed to step onto the national stage."

"That's what I figured. And she wasn't sure if that was what she wanted?"

"One day she came to me and told me about it. We met in a motel up in Westchester. She didn't know what to do. She said that if they had approached her before she met me she would have had no hesitation at all. But I had helped change her perspective and she wasn't sure if she could deliver what they expected of her."

"When was that?"

"That was the last time I saw her, about a week before she died."

"I thought you broke up earlier than that?"

"We did. But you know when it comes to love we're all just about sixteen. I knew it was a risk that I shouldn't take. But when she called and said she needed to talk, the prospects of one more encounter with this wonderful woman overwhelmed any sense I had."

The judge swiveled in his chair and looked out the window. "This area hasn't changed much since I began here in the seventies. I used to believe that I could make a difference, that maybe my being here would tip a few people's lives in a better direction."

"I'm sure that you have made a difference."

Thompson shrugged. "I'm not sure anyone does." He turned toward Lowell. "It's all going to hell in a hand-basket, isn't it?"

"Yes."

The judge shook his head. "I love this country. How did it happen so fast?"

"It didn't. The foundation has been crumbling for decades."

"I guess you're right. We were all so busy dealing with our day-to-day lives we never saw the decay until the base gave way. So what happens now? What does the astrology say about the next twenty years?"

"This is one of those times when humanity has to make a decision. Do we just go along the same path and wait for the inevitable results, or do we make a stand?"

"What do you think?"

Lowell sighed. "I think we will pay a heavy price for our past transgressions."

The judge nodded. He took a snapshot of Farrah from his shirt pocket. "This is the only picture I kept." He caressed it gently with his fingertips as he spoke. "She was a remarkable woman. I wouldn't have let this happen, if I had only known."

"You were not to blame for her death," said Lowell. "It was these men with their hidden agenda who put an end to her life."

"Still, if I had not gotten involved with her she might still be alive. In fact, she would probably be a senator. And even a conservative Farrah Winston is better than none."

He looked at the picture one more time and then returned it to his pocket. "I cannot thank you enough for keeping my name out of this. It would have ruined my marriage and ended my career."

"So now what?"

The judge leaned back and arched his fingers. "I'm announcing my retirement at the end of the month. I've had enough, and there's nothing more I can do. We are heading into a new world, and I agree with you that our nation will be shaken up for years to come."

"All the more reason to have someone like you in a position to help."

"No, not anymore. I've watched as America turned its back on everything I believed in. Years of lies and deceit at the highest levels of government and financial institutions have left me exhausted and frustrated. I haven't got the strength to keep fighting. We have a small house in Vermont on a lake. All I want to do is spend what time I have left with my wife. I will never finish mourning Farrah. But at least, thanks to you, I can do so in the privacy of my own thoughts."

Lowell stood.

"Would you do me one more favor?" Thompson stood to say goodbye.

"What's that?"

"If you do finally unravel this thing, will you please let me know who had Farrah killed?"

"Of course, your honor."

Chapter Forty-Two

When Lowell, Melinda, and Johnny arrived at the courthouse the next day a group of reporters had gathered outside.

A cacophony of shouted questions rained down on them as they ran the gauntlet. "Ms. Lowell, is it true that there is evidence that will exonerate your client?" "Who did it?" "Was it another judge?"

They went up to the judge's chambers on the fourth floor. Roland was there already.

When all the principals were seated, Melinda began.

"We were able to discover the identity of the person who killed Judge Farrah Winston."

"And was that person Johnny Colbert?" asked Harris, the D.A.

"No," she said, "it most certainly was not."

A TV monitor was rolled in and hooked up to Melinda's laptop computer. She hit play and the screen was filled with the sight of Lowell and the hit man's encounter. It was set to only show a few seconds before the man's confession, but there was enough for all to see the results of the violence that had preceded it.

The judge turned toward Roland. "Lieutenant, you have seen this entire video?"

"Yes. It was shown to me in its entirety by Mr. Lowell."

"And have you ascertained whether or not this is genuine?"

"I have. We went to the building where this altercation took place and found the body of the man on the tape. Then we went to a townhouse on East Thirty-eighth Street, where this man had been residing. We found plastique explosives and detonators identical to those that were used in the murder."

"Did you find any connection between this man and Johnny Colbert?" asked Harris.

"No. There is absolutely no evidence to tie them together."

"Then is there any way that the defendant was responsible for the death of Judge Farrah Winston?"

"I would have to say no, she in no way played a part in the victim's death."

"Mr. Harris," said the judge, "what say you on this matter?"

Harris was flummoxed.

"Mr. Harris?" repeated the judge.

"Your Honor, due to these facts that have come to light, the prosecution withdraws its complaint."

Outside, the crowd of reporters had grown appreciably. They swarmed around Johnny and Melinda. Lowell had gone out the back way to avoid the attention.

"How does it feel to be free?" "Did you really use astrology to crack this case?" "What will you do now, Johnny?"

Shouted questions flew from all directions, but this time, Melinda stopped and held up her hands. The crowd quieted.

"This has been a horrible time for my client, and she desperately needs her rest. I will make a short statement, and then we beg of you to leave us in peace.

"Johnny has been vilified and reprimanded repeatedly in the press. She has been called the worst of names, threatened and demonized, even before a judgment was declared. This is called conviction by hearsay. There have been no fewer than twenty death threats sent to her, as well as the horrible inaccuracies that have made their way onto blogs and Facebook. If we are to remain a civilized society in a time of instant gratification and worldwide communications, we must rise to a standard upon which such inventions and advancements can improve our culture, not destroy it.

"This case is an example of how easy it is to be accused of a crime and have the finger of circumstance pointed in your direction. This is still the greatest country in the world. We have a legal system that works, but it is flawed. Like everything else in America it favors the rich. Most people without means will never get the chance to have a competent defense. This case proves once again how important it is for people to have access to a good lawyer when they need one. And I'm glad to have had the chance to defend this innocent woman."

"Johnny, got anything to add?" asked one reporter.

"Yeah, it's good to be free."

"Ms. Lowell, Jane Goodman from CNN. Just one more question that's been bugging us all, if you don't mind. Did you really use astrology to help crack this case?"

"Yes, we did."

"But how can an intelligent person like you believe in that nonsense?"

Melinda's face grew red. She turned to the reporter. "Jane, I have been a student of astrology since I was nine. You have not. As you said, I am an intelligent person and have seen repeatedly what this wonderful ancient tool is capable of. Your ignorance on the subject is strikingly obvious. You know nothing about it, and I think you should learn something about what you ridicule beforehand. My father's astrological work has been documented for decades, and was invaluable in defending my client. Without the use of his talents in half a dozen ways, there would have been a catastrophic injustice. So before you use words like 'nonsense' do some homework. Some of the smartest people I have ever met are advocates of astrology.

"Now," said Melinda, grabbing Johnny's arm, "if you will all excuse us we have a dinner engagement."

Chapter Forty-Three

Lowell had called Julia when the case was dismissed and given her instructions for their celebration. Mort and Sarah greeted them enthusiastically at the door, and Andy came up after parking the limo.

A fire was roaring in the living room, and fluted glasses with freshly poured champagne were waiting. When everyone was settled, they each took a glass.

"The honor of first toast goes to my daughter," said Lowell, "the hero of the day."

Melinda raised her glass. "To the real hero of the day, justice, that rare and most elusive of guests."

They all drank.

"Can I make a toast?" asked Johnny.

"Most definitely," said Lowell.

She cleared her throat theatrically and began. "There is no way I can truly express what I feel. You were all just so wonderful to me. I just wanted to thank all of you. Melinda Lowell, brilliant attorney at law. David Lowell, the unusual but equally brilliant astrologer. And to everyone at the Starlight Detective Agency. May you go on to help many others who need you."

Cheers of "*here, here*" filled the room.

Dinner was one of Julia's best. It was a smorgasbord of delights, half vegetarian and half not. Lowell stuffed himself a little too much. He had to unbuckle his trousers, and he vowed this time to pull that paunch in. His life had depended on speed and timing in his recent skirmish and he just barely had enough. The next time he might not.

Tomorrow the gym.

◇◇◇

Lowell sat by the fire and put his feet up on the footstool. His leg was still quite sore and the heat felt comforting. He'd noticed that Johnny had tempered her drinking quite a bit. Now she was sipping a glass of red wine.

Johnny looked at David and Melinda with tears in her eyes. "I can't possibly thank you both enough. I could never rely on people my whole life, and you two strangers came along and saved me. I don't think I'll ever truly understand why, but I owe you both more than I could ever repay."

She wiped a tear off a cheek.

"Your freedom is thanks enough. What are you going to do now?" Melinda was sitting next to her father again. She realized that this close time together would return to old rhythms with the case over.

"I don't know. I guess I'll go back home tomorrow and try to put my apartment back together. Everything I own including my clothes has been destroyed. All I have are the things you bought me to wear to trial. My landlord has been trying to evict me ever since this all started. He went to court to argue that I don't deserve my rent-stabilized apartment because I was a murder suspect. I had to send a friend to housing court to ask for a delay in the case until I knew what was going to happen to me. What is it with me and courts all of a sudden? Now that I've been cleared, he's saying that I wrecked the place. I don't know what to do."

Lowell sipped his beer and watched the fire as it danced its waltz, sparkling here and there, like Hallowe'en glitter on a young girl's face. He had a great fondness for fireplaces from when he was newly married. He and his wife had little money; such was the way of an astrologer's life. He realized how lucky he was to have been able to use his skills on Wall Street, but that had taken a long, long time. Early in their marriage his wife's uncle had died and left her an old stone house near Woodstock, and the huge fireplace there had been a revelation. They would laugh and make love and fall asleep in front of the fire. How had his marriage gone off course? What should he have done differently? He looked at his beautiful daughter and realized something really wonderful had come from the union, and that was enough for him for now. Then he looked at this strange, beautiful bartender in his living room.

"Johnny, what would you do with your life if you had your choice?"

"I don't know. I've always had to work six nights a week just to make ends meet. I've never had time to give it much thought. If it paid enough and I could find a job, I guess I'd work with animals. I love animals, you know. But who's going to hire me without experience?"

Lowell nodded. They were silent for a while, watching the flames, all of them lost in their own thoughts.

Even in the warmth of fire, wine and close ones, Lowell's mind was churning. He often felt a severe physical letdown after a victory, but not this time. They were not out of danger yet.

Chapter Forty-Four

Before sunrise, Mort and Lowell were at work in the basement office. They were still working on the security upgrades for the house. It would take another few days to complete and the place was a jumble of cameras and wires. Lowell stepped over several pieces of equipment and settled into his chair.

"I'll get most of this done this week," said Mort. "I'm still waiting for some pieces from Switzerland. You should be up and running by Friday."

"Any luck uncovering that Purple Diamond thing?"

"A bit. Purple Diamond Industries has interests all around the world, always through some sort of holding company. They don't directly own anything. They have one in China, the Middle East, Africa, and just about everywhere. They are a private equity company put together for the purpose of investing in large land projects like Pilgrim's Cavern. There are exactly twenty shareholders."

"The same number on the list of investors in the launch of Winston's political career."

"Another coincidence."

"Exactly."

Lowell stood up and paced back and forth as he spoke, his right hand unconsciously tugging on his ponytail.

"So, Purple Diamond Industries, a group of rich and powerful conservative Republicans, puts together a multibillion dollar development plan in Pilgrim's Cavern, and then puts millions of dollars behind an unknown political entity to be appointed state senator, who winds up dead before she can be put into office."

"Seems that way."

"And then someone frames our client and makes numerous attempts to bury it, and us."

"What do you think?"

"I think the circle is close to completion."

Lowell had asked everyone to come to breakfast at nine.

"With the death of the murderer and Johnny's exoneration, I feel that the immediate threat has subsided sufficiently and everyone can return home, and the agency can resume its work downtown." The smiles around the table were caught up short when Lowell was quick to resume his pronouncement. "I would still ask that you be acutely aware of your surroundings and *please* call Andy for a ride, especially after dark."

Melinda held up the paper. "Did you see the *Post*? Your face is right on the cover."

"Yeah," said Johnny, "people really know who you are."

"I'm glad that more people are taking an interest in my work. But I could live without all the notoriety."

"Oh, get over it," said Johnny. "You're a rock star now and you should enjoy it while it lasts. Hey, they'll all be running up to you for autographs soon."

Lowell made a face. "Let's hope not. What a thought. Well, let's get packed and on our way. Andy will take everyone where they need to be, suitcases and all, later. For now, Mort, Sarah, its back to East Twenty-fourth."

◇◇◇

Lowell was feeding the turtles when the phone buzzed. "Melinda's on line one."

He was about to pick up the phone when Sarah suddenly shrieked. "Oh, my God!"

Lowell jumped out of his seat and was about to run out to her desk. "What is it? What happened?" he asked, expecting the worst.

"Ketchup," she screamed over the speakerphone, "on my white shoes!"

Lowell sat back down, his heart racing. Yes, things were returning to normal. He picked up the phone. "Hi, Melinda, everything all right?"

"Not really. I'm with Johnny. We went to her apartment and found that her landlord locked her out of her apartment."

"Isn't that illegal?"

"Certainly. I've filed papers and the courts have issued a warrant for his arrest. We should be able to get her back in by tomorrow, day after at the latest."

Lowell heard Johnny's voice. "I told you, you don't have to do this. I'll be fine. I just have to figure something out."

Melinda spoke to both of them. "No, you won't be fine unless we do something. There is nothing wrong with asking for help. We all need it sometimes."

"And then what? You think he's going to just let me live in peace after I had him arrested? My life is going to be hell."

"I hadn't thought of that. We can get the court to issue a follow-up warning."

"You don't get it, do you? I won't be safe, especially coming home from the bar late at night. You know, I think those two goons that ripped up my place were sent by him."

"I think you may be right. The same thought occurred to me."

Lowell jumped in from his side of the phone. "Tell Johnny to go back uptown to the townhouse. I have an idea."

Lowell clicked off then picked up the phone again and dialed his lawyer. "Hello, Bernie, it's David Lowell."

"What can I do for you David?"

"You know how you've been bugging me to diversify my holdings?"

"Don't tell me you're actually taking money out of the bank?"

"I'd like to buy something, and I need you to put the deal together. Price is not a concern."

"Sure, I can start right away. What is it you want to buy?"

After the phone call, Lowell reviewed a number of charts on his desk, called Mort a few times, and generally pivoted in his chair mulling over the case. After a few hours, he called Andy, asking him to bring Johnny by and pick him up.

Lowell and Johnny rolled up Second Avenue in the back of the limo. New Yorkers had broken out gloves and scarves for the first time, now that a late autumn chill had set in.

"Johnny, I may have a place for you to stay, if you want it."

"Where?"

"In Manhattan. The rent would be very reasonable, and there would be a job available as well, if you decided not to continue in the bar business. Are you interested?"

"Well, I'd like to know more about it. Bartending is the only thing I know how to do."

"Do you still want to do it?"

"No, I really hate it. There isn't a part of my body that doesn't hurt most all the time."

She turned her wrist, creating a loud cracking sound. "You hear that? That's from pouring a hundred thousand drinks. My knees hurt, that ankle I broke as a kid swells up sometimes where I can't walk. My back aches and I drink too much." She laughed. "Sounds like a hell of a job description, doesn't it?"

"I can't understand why you'd want to leave it," David grinned. "I tell you what, let's go take a look at the situation, and you can think about it before you decide. There's no commitment. Ah, here we are."

The limo pulled up in front of Cuddles and Puddles pet store.

Johnny peered through the car's glass. "What's this all about?"

"I am buying this building, along with the store. If it's going to remain a pet store, I'm going to need a new assistant manager. The old one quit. There's a vacant apartment on the second floor. You would also, of course, get a salary."

She stared at him.

"I've known the manager for years. He's a very nice guy who would be happy to teach you the business. And I think after running a bar for so many years you'll have no problem catching on. It'll take about a week for me to get possession of the building; in the meantime I'll put you up in a hotel. So, what do you say?"

Johnny kissed Lowell on the cheek. She tried to say something but couldn't.

"There is one catch," said Lowell, after the emotions had subsided.

"What's that?"

◇◇◇

The structure was old by New York standards, prewar brick. It served many functions for the community; civic meetings, daycare center, voting place, even distributing Thanksgiving dinner to those less fortunate. Tonight it was reserved for a special kind of meeting.

The room was in the basement. No sign announced its purpose, just a note tacked up that read: *Tonight's meeting is in room B.* After a moment they began to descend the stairs, Lowell leading the way. As they entered the hallway, there were two signs, each with an arrow pointing the way; room A was to the left and Room B to the right. The meeting was called for seven. They were just on time.

They entered the room and stood quietly in the back. There were about twenty or so people sitting on folding chairs. Some had coffee cups in hand. A few were reading or working on a laptop. Several were chatting.

A woman went up front and stood at the podium. The laptops, books and magazines closed, the room fell silent.

"Welcome everyone, I'm so glad to see so many of you here. I see we have some newcomers tonight." She looked at Johnny. "Would anyone like to introduce themselves?"

Johnny looked up at Lowell.

He smiled at her and nodded.

She raised her hand.

"Good. Why don't you come up here and say hello."

Johnny walked up to the front of the room and stood by the podium. The room was silent as she stared out at the strangers' faces.

"What do I do?" she whispered to Sally Rogers.

"Just say hello, tell them your first name and that you have a gambling problem."

She swallowed, cleared her throat and faced the crowd.

"Hello, my name…"

She stopped and looked over at David. He smiled and gave her a thumb's up.

"My name," she began again, "is Joanna. And I have a gambling problem."

Chapter Forty-Five

Lowell had asked Melinda, Sarah, and Mort to be at the office early. He fed the turtles as he gazed out the window at the Empire State Building.

"We know Farrah Winston was killed, and we know who actually did the murder. We know about the land deal in Utah, Winston's lovers, and her political plans, but that's it. I'm at a loss."

Lowell opened the top desk drawer and removed a small felt pouch. He pulled opened the drawer string and tipped the pouch, pouring three objects into his left hand.

"What that?" asked Sarah.

"These are astro-dice." He held them out. "There are three twelve-sided cubes. You will notice that on one there are the signs of the zodiac. On this second one there are the twelve heavenly bodies used in modern astrology, and on the third are the numbers one through twelve, to represent the houses in a horoscope."

"Boy, you sure do have a lot of toys," said the secretary. "How do they work?"

"You think of a single question and let the dice fall. The answer will give you a planet in a certain sign in a particular house. For example, if you were worried about your finances and threw Jupiter in the second house in Taurus, it would imply that money would be coming your way and not to worry. If, however, you threw Saturn in that house it would mean that your money issues were not over and that financial restraint was needed."

"Are they accurate?"

"Sometimes they are astonishingly right on the mark. Other times the question or the answer may be too vague to be of much use. I find that it has a lot to do with my mood at the time and how sharp my intuition is. But remember, I use many tools to achieve my goals. I primarily rely on astrology charts to find my answers and only use these devices as secondary tools. It seems to work best when I have already pinpointed the information I require through other investigative means."

He casually picked up the astro-dice and let them drop onto the table.

"The North Node in the 3rd House in Gemini."

"What does that mean?"

"It could mean a lot of things, but in this instance it certainly is saying *look into the details. The answer is in the little things.*"

He picked them up again and rolled them in his hand as he thought of his question. "How do I find the person responsible for the murders?"

He dropped the dice.

"Mercury in Cancer in the 4th House. Okay, now it's implying that the missing details may have something to do with a home."

He threw the dice a third time, and again it was Mercury, only this time in Virgo in the 7th House.

"What does that throw mean?"

"Mercury rules paperwork and Virgo deals with details. The 7th House is partnerships or legal contracts." He picked up the dice and threw them a few more times. Finally he placed them back in the pouch and put it back in the desk drawer.

"Done?" asked Melinda.

"They have already answered the question and are becoming redundant."

"What's the answer?" asked Sarah.

Lowell sat looking at a half dozen charts in front of him, his stone-like face reminiscent of his turtles' namesake. His eyes roamed from one chart to another and back again, searching for that one connection he might have missed; that singularity that would stand out and finally put all the pieces together.

But it wouldn't come.

He put the papers in a neat pile, stood up and stretched. "Oh, well, maybe it'll come to me later."

"Well," said Melinda, "it could be worse. You could have to deal with it on retrograde Mercury."

"What does that mean?" asked Sarah.

Lowell continued. "Several times a year the planet Mercury appears to go backwards in the sky for about three weeks at a time. Because Mercury rules communication and all paperwork, these are usually periods when many errors happen."

"As if we don't have enough to worry about," said Melinda.

"Actually, if it were in retrograde it could work to our advantage."

"How so?"

"Secrets often are revealed when this aspect occurs. The world slows down and gives us a chance to catch up on things. And if I remember correctly, Mercury was retrograde around the time Farrah Winston was murdered."

"Was it?"

He grabbed his astrology calendar and flipped back several weeks. "Mercury *was* in retrograde in the weeks leading up to the first murder. In fact, it only turned around two days before the event, the very day Johnny was in court. That means that the planning and preparation took place during that most annoying of times." David smiled broadly. "I think that's what the dice were trying to tell me."

"Translation?" Mort had been quiet until now. He had been watching Lowell closely.

"Blunders and oversights. Mistakes are common and often overlooked." said Lowell. "Things are very confusing and chaotic while Mercury is retrograde, and especially so as it changes direction."

He picked up a chart from his desk. "I wonder." He sat back down and pulled out several of the charts, opened the astrology computer program and started to enter data.

He chuckled. "Could it be so simple? Mort, I want you to find out what you can about the financial situation of someone. Get whatever you can regarding investments, bank statements, anything."

"Okay, who?"

He told him.

"This isn't going to be easy."

"I also want you to see if you can get me a copy of a certain document." He wrote down the information on a piece of paper and handed it to him. "I must have a physical copy, nothing less will suffice."

Mort looked at the paper. "How am I going to get a physical copy of this?"

Lowell smiled and raised his eyebrows. "As you put it so succinctly once, I didn't hire you for your looks."

"I'll try, but I can't promise anything. This may be a bit difficult to get."

"See what you can do."

"Do you mind my asking why?"

"Because I'll bet my bottom dollar that the person who signed it is responsible for all our misfortune. The devil *is* in the details. And this is one devil that I plan to send back to hell."

Chapter Forty-Six

Lowell entered the office building on Park a little after nine, took the elevator to the eighteenth floor and walked the few steps to the receptionist. She was a different girl than the one who had been working the last time he visited. The other was a blond, perky and playful, with a lilting musical voice and a Tinkerbelle twinkle in her eye. This one was an older brunette who gave off a no-nonsense aura. He preferred brunettes.

"David Lowell to see Mark Milford."

"Yes, sir," she said, in a husky Lauren Bacall voice. "Do you have an appointment?"

"No. But if you tell him I'm here, I'm certain he will find a few moments to see me. Just say it's about Pilgrim's Cavern."

She looked at him with uncertainty, those eyes studying him, exuding sexuality, without the slightest intent.

Must be a Scorpio, thought Lowell.

Finally she picked up the phone and buzzed her boss. "There's a Mr. Lowell here to see you...no, he doesn't have an appointment. He said it's regarding something called Pilgrim's Cavern. He said you would know what it was about...yes, sir."

"Mr. Milford will see you right away." She seemed impressed.

Milford's secretary came out and escorted him into the office.

"Mr. Lowell, how nice to see you again. Was there some unfinished business regarding the Winston case?" He didn't rise from his chair. Lowell didn't sit.

"The Winston case? Is that how you think of it? It wasn't so long ago in this very office that you tried to convince me of a flowering relationship cut short by the tragic death of your lover."

"Please don't take me for indifferent."

"I don't. I take you for a cold, calculating murderer."

Milford showed no sign that he had heard him. He got up and walked over to the bar where he poured a glass of orange juice. He took a long sip and put the glass down.

"Can I get you something?"

Lowell smiled. *I would require a food taster,* he thought, remembering how he duped Larry Rosen with the drugged lime slice. "No, thank you."

Milford shrugged. "So, what makes you think I'm a murderer?"

"You are familiar with Pilgrim's Cavern?"

"I've heard of it."

"What do you know about it?"

"Only that it's a plan to build a first-class resort in the Utah Mountains."

"It's in a rather isolated area for a resort, wouldn't you say?"

"It isn't a Holiday Inn."

"It also isn't really a resort, is it? It's more like a gold plated Noah's ark, wouldn't you say?"

"I believe that its proximity to the caverns does apparently add an element of protection."

"And what do you know about Purple Diamond Industries?"

"They represent a group of international financiers who comb the globe looking for long-term investments, mostly in property."

"Has your law firm ever done work for them?"

"I believe we may have some minor dealings with the P.D.I. group. I'd have to do some research to find out."

The man took a large cigar from a humidor, put it to his ear and rolled it between his fingers. Satisfied, he took a small clipper and cut the end off. Then he picked up what Lowell assumed correctly was a solid gold lighter and lit the cigar, twirling it to assure an even smoke.

"Cigar?"

Lowell shook his head.

"I did a little research of my own," said Milford. "I apologize for my attitude at our first meeting. It seems you are quite a wealthy man. Self-made, unlike myself. As I understand it, most of your money came as a result of trading oil, gold, and other commodities over the past decade. Capitalism in its most primal form. You are obviously a man of some intelligence to have accrued so substantial a fortune. And in so short a time."

Lowell modestly bowed his head.

"You interest me, Mr. Lowell. That is why I agreed to see you. I believe an individualist like yourself may be able to understand the bigger picture. In many ways this is a brave new world. It is a time in man's history of unprecedented wealth and expansion when individuals have accrued fortunes of such proportions that a few men can change the world. Kings and emperors never dreamed of the power that ordinary businessmen now hold."

"And how about the financial mess we're in right now? We seem to be heading deeper into a depression."

"Just a blip on the screen."

"Is that all the 1930s were to your family?"

He puffed on the cigar. "Families such as mine do not suffer during downturns in the economy. We flourish."

"If you are so confident about the future, why build a multi-billion dollar bomb shelter?"

"Some of our clients may not be as optimistic about the future as I am. If they wish to invest in such a project, our job is to aid them in every way possible."

"Well, this time I think you've gone above and beyond the call of duty."

Lowell stood up and walked to the window. It was nine-thirty in the morning, and traffic on Park Avenue was moving along steadily. He looked uptown at the endless row of skyscrapers with their thousands of bankers, lawyers, and businessmen willing to use any means and anyone to increase their personal fortunes.

The American game, now gone sour. "Let me tell you what I think happened." He turned to face Milford.

The man sat silently, blowing smoke rings in groups of three.

"You, like so many others, overextended your resources over the past few decades. The crash of '08 was when the bottom finally fell out for you, isn't it? My research shows that over the past few years a number of your high-end clients have defaulted on their debts to your firm. Given bad investments, the decline of equity in your stock portfolio and an untenable extravagant lifestyle, you are so overleveraged that I doubt if you can even pay the interest on your outstanding debts. And my guess is that most, if not all, of your family's fortune is tied up in your investments.

"One of your clients, Purple Diamond Industries, has a long-term commitment for investments in certain projects, including the development of Pilgrim's Cavern. Your fee for setting up the deal would be quite sizable and could get you out of the hole, perhaps without your family ever finding out. But it had to get done this year, or it would be too late for you. You can barely afford the interest on your loans, and if it went into committee it might very well never get completed. The project was moving along nicely, and everything was just fine. The governor was on board, as was a majority of the state senate. And then something happened you couldn't possibly have foreseen. One of those senators had a massive coronary while eating a two pound sirloin steak. The governor had to choose a replacement quickly, and you had to make sure that choice would favor the Pilgrim's Cavern project, or you would be bankrupt."

Milford puffed on his cigar, seemingly unfazed by Lowell's accusations.

"You must have been beside yourself searching for the proper candidate before the governor picked someone unsuitable. Then somebody mentioned Farrah Winston, an attractive, intelligent woman from an ultraconservative family in that state with roots deep in the Republican Party. You did your research, liked her background and, realizing that time was not on your side, you quietly brought her to the attention of your business associates.

They agreed to back her next year for U.S. Senate and to guarantee her continued career through large cash donations. As long as she was willing to spend this year in the state senate and go along with the Pilgrim's Cavern project.

"She was discreetly approached by the governor's office and agreed to accept the appointment in the state legislature. Your research showed that she was too honest to accept any strings attached to the job, but you were confident she would vote the right way when the time came. Several issues were discussed with her, including the Pilgrim's Cavern project. But unbeknownst to you her attitude had been changing. She began to show interest in some uncomfortable issues, such as the environmental impact this would have on the region.

"Nothing could stop you. Except maybe a fiery state senator who had recently had her eyes opened. How am I doing so far?"

Milford said nothing.

"You needed to find out for yourself, so you planned an *accidental* meeting where you swept her off her feet. Just as you had feared, her attitude was anything but cooperative. Not knowing you were involved with Purple Diamond Industries, she told you that she was planning to thoroughly investigate the Pilgrim's Cavern project once she was appointed.

"The governor, like most men, was charmed by Farrah Winston and very happy with the choice. He is basically an honest man who pretty much follows the party line. He was a fan of the Pilgrim's Cavern project, but not at the cost of Farrah's appointment.

"The announcement was only days away. You panicked. You needed someone in her office to help you, so you somehow recruited Larry Rosen. He was a fanatic, and you played to his hatreds and fears. You convinced him that Farrah was a stone's throw from the presidency and that she represented a threat to his way of life. You hired that hit man to kill her once Rosen had given you a patsy in my client. Once Farrah was dead, you were able to get George Ogden, a lackey who you knew would follow orders, appointed in her place. Just to make sure there were no loose ends, you decided to eliminate the problem once and for all on Riker's, but your thugs missed. And when I got too close, you had him try to kill me. He failed, so you decided to clean up your mess starting with Rosen."

"You have a very vivid imagination."

"Has anyone in your family ever been poor?"

"Not since the fifteenth century, when my ancestors pulled themselves out of the rubble of plague-infected Europe and began a profitable shipping business in Venice. My family has been wealthy for five hundred years. So you see the term nouveau riche is relative. To me it describes the Rockefellers and the Vanderbilts."

"And you think it's okay to take land from those who already live there?"

"The stronger have always taken from the weaker."

"I see. So we've replaced the chariots and lances with corporate jets and checkbooks, is that it?"

"That's the way of the world. I'm surprised a man of your wealth and position doesn't understand that."

"How does it feel to be the one to end a family legacy that has lasted half a millennium?"

A small crevice developed on his forehead, but Milford said nothing.

"You are responsible for the deaths of Farrah Winston and Larry Rosen, and I will see to it that you are held accountable."

"All you have are suppositions, innuendo, and guesses. There is nothing to tie me to Farrah's death, nor the Pilgrim's Cavern project."

"I'm sure that if someone were to dig deep enough into your paperwork, they would find that this firm was more connected to Pilgrim's Cavern than you let on."

"Do you expect me to give you access to my files?"

"No. That privilege will be reserved for the courts."

"Mr. Lowell, my clients include two congressmen, a senator, and an ex-governor. Your threats do not impress me. And even if you did find some lunatic judge to agree to examine my firm's dealings, I employ fifty-six lawyers who each handle hundreds of cases a year. I couldn't possibly know about them all. As I said, we may very well have had some minor dealings with someone associated with this project, but that would be the extent of the connection."

"I'm sure you could explain it away easily enough."

"That's right."

"And you personally would never be connected to this affair."

"Absolutely not."

"You see, the mistake both the police and I made was assuming your alibi was solid. After all, you were on the phone with the victim and the investigation proved that the bomb was not set off by a cell phone. So the phone call was both an alibi and confirmation of the deed."

Milford shrugged. "I was on the phone with my lover planning our dinner date when she was killed. Your accusations are slanderous, and if you repeat them to anyone else I may be forced to take legal action."

"When I'm finished, if you still wish to sue me for defamation of character, I'll give you my lawyer's card."

Milford's got up and freshened his drink.

"Details," said Lowell, "it's all in the details. When your killer came to New York to fulfill his contract, he needed a place to stay where he could come and go without attracting the attention of hotel employees or neighbors in an apartment building. After all, he didn't exactly blend into a crowd. You couldn't put him up anywhere that would be connected with you or any of your business associates, so you rented him a townhouse."

"You can't prove any of this."

"You really should study astrology. It can help you avoid many of the little pitfalls that bedevil us. Had you known that Mercury was in retrograde when you planned the crime, you may have been able to take precautions."

Milford smirked as he sat back down.

"It must have been quite hectic that day, your investors screaming for a resolution, the governor unknowingly just about to make an announcement that would ruin your life. You had a hundred things running through your mind, all at the same time. And dozens of little troublesome details to take care of.

"You couldn't trust anyone to know that you were directly involved with your lover's murderer, so having one of your flunkies take care of things was out of the question. You probably weren't paying attention, or maybe you figured it would never come out in a million years, nobody would ever untangle the labyrinth you had so carefully created, so you must have unconsciously just scribbled a signature on the bottom, as you do a hundred times a day, and then mailed it back. Did you know that it is very difficult to disguise your script? And I doubt that you even bothered to try."

He took a document out of the envelope and dropped it on the desk in front of Milford. "That is your handwriting, isn't it? It shouldn't be hard for an expert to determine."

Milford just stared.

"How will you explain to the police why your handwriting is on the lease to a townhouse where Judge Winston's murderer was staying?"

Milford opened his mouth but nothing came out.

The intercom buzzed. Milford seemed not to hear it.

It buzzed again.

"Yes, Michele," he snapped, "what is it?"

"There's a Lieutenant Roland here to see you.

Chapter Forty-Seven

Snow fell last night, as pure as a baby's soul. No footprints at all, no mistakes to erase.

If only we could walk through life without disturbing it, thought Lowell as he went out the kitchen door, coffee cup in hand, and stood on the back porch gazing onto the pristine carpet. His actions had killed a man. It wasn't supposed to end that way. This was something he would carry with him forever, long past this lifetime, so he believed. But it had been necessary to protect him and his loved ones.

Or had it?

It was one of those rare and sudden storms brought on by the Gemini full moon, all gaudy and flamboyant. It fell on Friday, a white weekend, and would charm the city, as only the first snowfall of the year could. By February the snow would have long ago lost its seductive powers.

Maybe he could have played his hand another way. Maybe, if he had taken Lieutenant Roland into his confidence earlier, they could have shaken the truth from the hit man. But he knew in his heart that wouldn't have been the case. And so he took the weight onto his karmic shoulders and accepted it.

A little more than a week had passed since his confrontation with Milford, yet how much had already changed. Once the public became aware of it, the governor was forced to cancel the Pilgrim's Cavern project. It would be years before another attempt would be made at stealing the town, but Lowell knew in his heart that it was only a matter of time before someone did. The world was shrinking, and the rules were changing rapidly.

As for Milford, his life lay in ruins and he faced many years in prison. Lowell was not surprised to hear that, just two days ago, Milford had decided to take the coward's way out with the aid of a bottle of whiskey and a handful of pills. Lowell would not mourn the loss.

He went back into the kitchen and sat by the counter. The house was quiet. He could hear Julia's TV in the distance tuned, as always, to her soaps. He got up from the stool and walked into the den. Maybe he'd build a fire and have a cup of tea. How Dickensian.

And I'll throw a shawl on and sit in a rocking chair waiting for death. No, thank you, he said to himself.

He walked back into the kitchen and opened the fridge. He took out an apple, then changed his mind and put it back. It was too quiet, that's what was bothering him. He picked up the phone and dialed.

"Hey."

"Hi, Dad."

"I was wondering if you'd like to come up for the weekend and play in the snow. You're welcome to bring anyone you want."

"I'd love to. Let me see how much work I get done the rest of today."

"Bring the work up with you. You can use the den and work by the fire."

"That sounds nice. No promises but let me call you later this afternoon."

"Okay."

He hung up and walked down to the office and sat looking out the window. He didn't like winter, never did. Even as a child it was a nuisance, dressing and undressing, fending off snowball laden bullies and slippery sidewalks. And now in middle years the energy it took to deal with the cold and snow made it less pleasant each winter. Eventually, he supposed, he would move someplace warm, at least for the winters.

He'd tried living other places, small towns, other cities, even tried Miami once. But everything paled compared to New York. There was no other place in the world like Manhattan Island, even in a depression.

Even in winter.

He picked up the phone and made a call.

Ten minutes later Andy was waiting in front. He and Lowell nodded to each other knowingly as Lowell got in the back of the limo.

"Where to, boss?"

"Bermuda," replied the astrologer, as he settled into his private, portable sanctum.

To receive a free catalog of Poisoned Pen Press titles, please contact us in one of the following ways:

Phone: 1-800-421-3976
Facsimile: 1-480-949-1707
Email: info@poisonedpenpress.com
Website: www.poisonedpenpress.com

Poisoned Pen Press
6962 E. First Ave. Ste. 103
Scottsdale, AZ 85251